They Walk With Us

John T. Mainer

The Troth

2015

"Offered and Taken" was originally published in Idunna #90 (Winter 2011).
"The Nom Nom Gnome" was originally published in *Idunna* #96 (Summer 2013).
"Helm of Awesome" was originally published in *Idunna* #101 (Autumn 2014).
"Lessons of a Hammer" was originally published in *Idunna* #103 (Spring 2015).

Published by The Troth
24 Dixwell Avenue, Suite 124
New Haven, Connecticut 06511
http://www.thetroth.org/

ISBN-13: 978-1-941136-08-9 (paperback), 978-1-941136-09-6 (hardcover)

Cover images: Ancient helmet from Grave XII, Vendel, Uppland, Sweden, courtesy of the Swedish Historical Museum, object 120459; http://kulturarvsdata.se/shm/object/html/120459 Image released under Creative Commons CC-BY 2.5 SE.

Modern helmet: Danish M96 Combat helmet, © Lasse Jensen, 2005. Image released through Wikimedia Commons.

Troth logo designed by Kveldulf Gundarsson, drawn by 13 Labs, Chicago, Illinois

Cover design: Ben Waggoner

Typeset in Palatino 18/14/11/9

It sounds like a simple concept. Our ancestors lived in a far different world than we did. In the ages before the religions of the book, we did not accept a division between the spiritual world and the physical one. We did not accept that the divine was something you could only seek beyond this world, or touch only beyond this life. This world belonged to the living and the dead; it was filled with spirits, not all of whom had bodies. Wonder and horror were all around us, and yet nothing was beyond our ability to deal with, for our ancestors, and our relationships built over time with the wights or spirits of the places we dwelled, and with those greater spirits who guided our people and whom we now like to fit neatly inside the label of gods, frequently shared this world with us.

To read Greek lore, their gods came to earth like thunderbolts, and the earth shook with their passage. For a group of gods that demanded sacrifice simply to placate them, this probably made sense, and certainly was an understandable model for those who would later follow Christianity, whose god also was big on "placate or else" as a working relationship.

Our own gods were vastly more complicated, far more subtle, and far more interested in stirring the pot and meeting us at important forks in the road or turning points to give us the opportunity to have choices of either greater good, or greater disaster as outcome. The gods walked among us in the lore as agents of change, as instigators, inspiration and catalysts. Are they done? Or do they walk with us still? Did they ever stop moving amongst us, offering us a whisper in the dark, a nudge at the crossroads? Or did we simply stop listening, or at least forget whom we were listening to? In the many of the stories in our lore, the role of the gods is inferred, is suggested, but rarely stated. The teller would imply and the audience would properly smile and nod, either forced to consider the possibility of a more than mortal involvement, or at least consider their choices and consequences in the context of their spiritual and moral beliefs, rather than their simple day to day utilitarian expediency.

Is that the purpose of the gods walking among us? To shine a light on our choices, on our opportunities, and to perhaps let us see ourselves through their eyes, and perhaps, see a little of their truths in this world we stumble through. I like to think so.

Our ancestors used story and myth to teach their worldview, to teach their children how to ask the right questions, and how to judge the choices the characters made so that in doing so they could learn to make better choices themselves. Wonder and horror filled the stories, mirth and madness, joy *and suffering, for all these things were part and parcel of the world of our ancestors, and thus part of the lessons they left behind.*

The best definition of myth I have ever heard is simply this "Lies that teach truths." What follows then is a collection of lies, and a collection of truths. Oddly enough may of the stories that you will read here spring from real life, the way the best stories do. Many of the events depicted did indeed happen, although I am not even trying to tell the story as it happened, so much as the tale that grew from it, to tell the truth learned in it. When I was a soldier, we would call such tall tales "No shit" stories, as we would begin each tale with "No shit" and everyone would laugh and be prepared to take everything with a grain of salt, but at the same time, these stories were the way we dealt with what actually did happen, and each of them rang with truth for those with the ears to hear.

To be a heathen means to live in the world that is, and accept it for what it is. We learn to look the darkness in the eye and accept it; we learn to love the light and sun, even while knowing the dark too is a part of us. We crave peace even as we celebrate conflict. We each strive to be free individuals, unique and strong, even as we deal with the soul-deep hunger to belong, and soul-crushing fear of loneliness. Heathenry teaches you to accept what you learn about the world, as it teaches you to accept what the world teaches you about yourself. The process of learning is sometimes funny, sometimes tragic, and sometimes flat-out interesting. So too are the stories.

Contents

Chapter 1: Sacrifice

Njord's Doughnut

Sacrifice: the act of making sacred, of offering either a physical thing, or an act done with the intent of pleasing some wight, be it a spirit of a place, an ancestor, or the gods. Our ancestors believed in building a reciprocal gifting relationship with the spirits that shared the lands and waters with them, and with the gods whose favour or luck could impact their success and even survival. An intelligent and pragmatic people, they practiced sacrifice for reasons that made sense to them, and received results which they found sufficient to continue the practice for centuries.

Although my service was infantry, I now find myself building boats for a living; passing in a sense from Odin's realm into Njord's. Commerce and the sea were his, and learning his ways has been an eye opener. The men who go down to the sea are superstitious as a group, even as they are harshly pragmatic.

Dave worked with boats, putting in engines and self-righting systems, as well as taking the new boats to sea trials to test the thousand modifications that each Navy, Coast Guard, and police department seemed compelled to add. While he was close to a work-a-holic, he still found time for his second wife and child (a lesson learned from losing the first wife). Sitting at the kitchen table at dinner, his daughter Alexis asked him about Njord.

"Is this some of your mom's witchy stuff?" Dave asked with his trademark tact. While his wife was a practicing pagan, Dave was more of a pragmatist, believing half of what he saw, little of what he was told, and trusting only what he'd proven would work for him.

Alexis rolled her eyes at her father's bluntness, and replied with the patience of a person addressing a new and not particularly bright puppy, or a woman talking to a man:

1

"No, dad, this is school stuff. You remember the whole cultural heritage project?"

Since Dave had totally forgotten, but had little doubt he'd been told, probably a few times, he nodded sagely and dragged up what he remembered. His family had been at sea for centuries, sometimes with the Navy, sometimes running rum to the States during prohibition, even whaling in the North. While he was not superstitious, the men who went down to the sea in fragile wooden ships, where wind and wave determined if you reached home alive, even in peacetime, often were, and the tales caught his interest when he was a child. "Right, Njord. He was the chief of the Vanir, the god of the sea."

Alexis looked confused, and countered, "I thought that was Ran."

Dave nodded and repeated, "Because the sea is a lady, and the lady's a bitch."

Something his father had always repeated. Seeing his wife's glare at his language, he decided to push on before she could chime in.

"Ran was the dark face of the sea, the deep depths, the sudden storm, the wrathful sea. She casts her nets for men and ships, and dragged them down. No one really wanted her attention."

He thought some more and then continued.

"Njord was different. Njord cared. Njord was the god not only of the sea, but of trade. Njord brought prosperity through hard work and daring. You called to Njord if you made your living on the sea, for the wrong wind could shear your sails, shiver your mast, the wrong waves could swamp you, or drive you far off course just to not get smashed. You called on Njord for fish luck, for whale luck, for wind luck and gentle waves.

"I think the waves were his daughters," Dave paused, thinking about it. "Although I think he married a mountain goddess or something, so I don't know how that worked. In the days when you had no compass or GPS, no radar or depth sounder, no electronic charts, no radio, no self-righting systems or dry-suits, the sea used to kill a lot of people. There is a reason sailors used to sacrifice to Njord before and after every trip. Out there, sometimes you survived on luck, and a little at the right time could save your life. Now we don't have to worry about that; we have better ships, and if you get in trouble, you can always call the Coast Guard."

Alexis thought about it for a while, and then asked her father:

"Aren't you doing a sea trial tomorrow? Shouldn't you give an offering to Njord for luck?"

Dave chuckled, shaking his head.

2

"That's your mother's thing. Besides, I'm not doing a sea trial, I'm just towing the new Japanese cabin boat out for a self-righting test. We'll sink her, use the airbag to flip her back up, and tow her back to shore without breaking a sweat."

He smiled complacently. They had done it a hundred times, it really was no big deal. Alexis and his wife shared a look, but Dave missed it as he headed to the den to catch the hockey game.

Saturday dawned without much promise. The good weather that had held for mid-December seemed to be fleeing, and cold, grey, nastiness was sweeping in on cold winds from the north. Dave put on his dry suit while listening to Troy complain about the upcoming test.

"I dunno, Dave," Troy said seriously. "The cabin on this thing is huge, it's like twice as deep as the keel. When this thing goes over, it's like an iceberg. Plus all the electronics are on top of the cabin, where you really don't want the weight."

Dave nodded; all this was true. The customer had made so many changes to the specs that this was almost a new boat. What really bugged him were the changes to the rope-guard where they mounted the self-righting airbag. The cylinder was over-pressured for North American regulations, but legal in Japan, and the airbag had been mounted on a bolt on flange, rather than directly on the rope guard like they usually did. The engineer swore it would work. Of course, the engineer wasn't towing it out to sea and sinking it to find out. That was Dave's job.

The Japanese boat was the dark orange of a rotting pumpkin, about as unattractive as you could make it. It sliced cleanly through the water as it was towed behind the predatory low sea-green hull of the Canadian Navy standard test boat. It was time to go play on the water before the weather hit. The radar was painting a storm front about an hour out, and the radio was broadcasting a small craft advisory. Not a problem; he was riding the Navy's version of the Coast Guard rescue boat, with better electronics and much better engines. Who needs luck, when you've got technology!

When they got into the Straits of Georgia, the seas were running about two meters, making the boats cant back and forth like a funhouse while Troy rigged the guide lines on the test boat: lines to help the boat flip back if the airbag failed. Dave opened his lunch kit to take out the sandwich he had packed for himself, and to pour some hot coffee. He looked down in surprise to see a green- and blue-covered jelly-filled doughnut wrapped in wax paper, with a tag on it that read:

NJORD'S DOUGHNUT. FOR LUCK ON THE TEST.

Dave was still shaking his head when Troy came over to see what he was laughing at, and Dave had to explain about Njord, and the sacrifice before voyages. Troy wasn't as quick to dismiss it.

"I dunno man, I don't go on these tests without my lucky rabbit's foot. I mean, sure, we build these things like race-cars, but between our customers and our engineers, I'm surprised they haven't forgotten to put a bottom on one yet."

It was true; there had been a whole lot of changes in this boat, and sometimes Dave didn't think anyone had really taken a look at the whole thing since they started changing the different bits of it. He still didn't believe in luck. Taking a big bite of Njord's doughnut, he told Troy,

"You don't see a lot of rabbits at sea, Troy. Lucky rabbits don't end up chopped up for key-chains, and we have a boat to sink, so enough about luck, and go sink me an ugly pumpkin." Dave watched the approaching squall line, and determined that they had better finish the test, and get back to shore. With waves looking to crest five meters at the storm's edge, it was no sea to be towing a boat in. He turned to watch the ugly pumpkin Japanese boat turn turtle, and settle keel up in the heavy seas. With a sigh, he put down the last half of Njord's doughnut and pushed the airbag remote to self-right the test boat.

That is when lessons on sea luck began.

The seas were definitely getting higher, and that probably spelled the doom of a system that had one too many modifications already. The ship was sliding broadside down a wave trough when the airbag deployed. Designed to fire just off centre to start the ship tipping, the airbag actually countered the tilt of the wave, letting the bag inflate directly under the boat, catching the full sideways force of the angry sea against its sail like bulk. The overpressured cylinder overcame the firing head that was supposed to control the airbag's inflation speed. Instead of exploding like a wave that would toss the boat back upright, it exploded like a depth charge that punched it momentarily out of the water, before crashing back, the bolted flange tore off the frame on the cabin top, and the great airbag was left dragging behind the cabin like a pontoon, simultaneously trapping the boat on its back, and making a great sea anchor with its parachute-like drag.

"Fudge puppets," Dave cursed, using the child friendly version of cursing he'd had to develop when he had children. The line that Troy had worked around the frame to help tip the boat back manually was snared in the self-righting bag itself. He would have to try to tow the whole ungainly mass back to shore—or cut his losses, and the tow rope, to leave the boat to the storm, and write off months of work and the better part of half a year's profits.

Bringing the massive engines online, his transom was pulled low in the water as the lean predatory boat strained to pull its damaged partner from the storm-tossed seas. It was like watching a porpoise trying to tow a sideways grey whale. The big cabin boat and its pontoon-like airbag turned broadside in the following seas and wallowed like a drowning pig, mocking the efforts of the big engines to power her to shore. Dave looked at the approaching squall line on the radar, and the distance to port, and didn't like his odds much. "So much for my rabbit's foot," said Troy. "It's going to take a whole lot of luck to get out of this one without calling mama for help," he said, pointing to the Coast Guard radio on the console. Dave frowned, because if he declared an emergency with a tow, they would tell him to drop a buoy and cut the line. That was the smart thing to do. Maybe it was time for something crazy instead.

Looking seriously at the half doughnut, and its sign to Njord, he considered. Troy followed his gaze to the doughnut, and began nodding.

"Do it man, I don't feel like swimming today."

Dave picked up his doughnut and went to the railing. Holding the rope lines on the side tube he spoke matter-of-factly to the heaving seas. "Njord, first of the Vanir, luck bringer, sea lord, we who ride the sea roads offer you this doughnut in return for your gifts of sea luck, for the shelter of your fair daughters the bright waves, that we may see our home ports again."

Dave was somehow unsurprised when he threw the sea-green doughnut out to sea, only to have a rogue wave rise and snap it from the air like a Major League midfielder catching a line drive. Troy was watching, wide-eyed and thoughtful, as Dave crossed the deck to grab hold of the wheel. When Troy began shouting, Dave looked back to see two converging waves closing on their wallowing charge, easily as high as their radar mast.

Dave spun the wheel hard and rammed the throttles home to see if he could ride out their force. Considering the dead weight they were still towing behind them, he didn't figure it would work, but the sea doesn't forgive people who don't do the little things right, so even as the waves closed he pulled the boat around to run before them.

When the waves hit the Japanese boat, it rolled like the Titanic in reverse. The force of the wave snapped the towline tight, halting the boat keel down, but wallowing with a hold full of water. Once upright, the sensors in the self-righting bag emptied the airbag, letting it deflate as so much cloth to drag behind the boat. The two waves folded around the lead boat like the closing palm of a giant jade hand, lifting them gently, then pushing them forward with soft authority. As the lead boat heaved forward, the water slammed to the back of the empty Japanese boat, and pushed out its scuppers, allowing it to rise higher in the water, and letting both boats start to pick up speed. As they began to move faster, the bow came up on both boats, and water streamed from the scuppers of the Japanese boat until it was cutting through the waves like a ship, not a wallowing hog. Troy came up with a grin, and looked Dave in the eye and said, only partly joking, "Looks like you owe somebody a half doughnut, dude!"

Dave nodded slowly and replied, "Looks like I owe somebody a whole new bloody doughnut."

Once the two boats were stowed on their trailers, and they had pulled their trucks up to the marina for a warmup coffee, the two men wandered over to the doughnut stand. The two men exchanged glances. There were two sprinkled, jelly filled doughnuts. Surrounded by the garish decorations of December, these two were the same horrible pumpkin shade of their problem boat. Dave pointed to one, while Troy silently indicated the other. Without a word, they strode out from the marina and onto the dock. Reaching the end, they paused to look at the windswept winter sea. Dave looked out at the crashing waves and shuddered to think how today might have gone, if the waves hadn't slapped their test boat upright. "Njord, my daughter was right, I owed you a doughnut. We needed your sea luck, and the help of your wave-daughters to get back. Take this doughnut and my thanks."

Troy, being less familiar with pagan rituals, just tossed his out as well, saying simply, "Cheers, man!"

As they walked back towards their trucks, Troy tossed his rabbit foot in the garbage. Turning to Dave, he shouted:

"Next time, Njord gets his doughnuts on the way out, right?"

"Damned straight!" Dave shouted back.

Sure he wasn't superstitious, but it was good to have friends you could count on at sea.

Nodding one last time to Njord, he turned his truck away from the sea and back to work.

It was about being practical.

Draupnir's Delicious Doughnuts

The Hávamál *is an interesting work. The sayings of the High One are deemed to be inspired by, or at least accepted by the ancestors to be in keeping with, the wisdom of Odin: Hár, the High One. Oddly for a god remembered primarily for his martial aspects, the warrior chieftain, the Hávamál is focused most strongly on setting forth what we call the "Laws of Hospitality", or the definition of duties between host and guest, between friends and family, between people both honest and false, friend and enemy. Equally divided between teaching you how to build and maintain positive relationships, and how to protect yourself from bad and or dangerous ones, the Hávamál carries with it a potent reminder of how important the smallest gestures of welcome, of generosity, and hospitality can be. "With half a loaf, and half filled cup, full friend found" we are told.*

In modern ages, mankind rediscovered the magic of "paying it forward" with the custom that Canada seems to enjoy of paying for the coffee and doughnut of the person behind you in drive through. Through such random acts of kindness, through such little gifts, we brighten the lives of others, and motivate the best of them to offer a gift for a gift, to someone else, and thus spread the magic of hospitality.

Lord of hospitality, Odin is also the keeper of oaths, so his ring Draupnir is not simply an item of wealth and power, it is a symbol of his leadership. Draupnir is not simply an oath ring, but a gifting ring, as it nightly duplicates itself nine times to allow Odin to be ever generous. Taken together the aspects of hospitality, generosity, and leadership can indeed be expressed through the gift of a golden ring. The doughnut.

Not for nothing is the bulk of the Hávamál about the use of gifts to foster and strengthen the bonds between people, for as it says, "With gifts a man should brighten his friends". We grow strong and healthy when we grow together. Sometimes to come together requires a helpful nudge from outside, by one who knows better than we, what we need.

For those who are not familiar with Heathen symbols, the Valknut, or three interlocking triangles is a symbol of Odin, most commonly worn by those marked as his own.

There was a new coffee shop on the way into work today. I had driven this road a thousand times before, and never noticed it under construction. Out of the fog it appeared: a lit neon sign advertised Draupnir's Delicious Doughnuts. Its sign was a cool interlinking of three D's. looking really familiar. I'm sure after my coffee, I will remember what that sign reminds me of.

It was Wednesday, arguably the least wonderful morning of the week, I tended to look at is as hump day. Sure, the last weekend is just a fading memory, but you are almost in sight of the next one. I liked to bring my crew doughnuts on random Wednesdays; Odin made a big deal about hospitality, and a little gesture at midweek often brightened them up.

As I pulled into the drive through to order my coffee, I saw the picture of a shining golden ring, an unbroken arc of warmth and richness that called out to me, and made my stomach grumble about another day of only coffee. I opened my mouth to order my coffee, and instead found myself saying:

"Half a loaf, and half filled cup, full friend found."

Hearing the line from the Hávamál come out as my morning coffee order assured me that this Wednesday was going to be both long and weird, but before I could correct myself, a heard a laugh and a matronly voice replied warmly:

"Draupnir Special coming up, please drive through."

Wondering what a Draupnir Special was, I drove past the smiling golden-haired woman taking the orders, and to the smiling greybeard at the window till. He took my money and handed me a box of doughnuts and a piping hot triple-triple (although I can't recall telling anyone how I took it). As I put my coffee and doughnuts away, I asked what the Draupnir Special was. Turning to face the clerk, I was momentarily shocked by the scars on his face, but his ready grin quieted me.

"One of these doughnuts is a little special." He winked his good eye as I drove away.

At work, my mood restored by the awesome coffee, I proceeded to put the dozen doughnuts on the main table at work. The first of my grumbling fellow managers staggered in, stopped and brightened considerably at the sight of the doughnuts, and then snagged one with a grin. As he walked away happily munching on the ring of baked golden goodness, he threw me a happy wave. One by one, my grumbling staff staggered in, saw the doughnuts and grabbed one. The men saluted with the doughnuts as they escaped with their loot, the women made it clear that they really didn't want or need such calorie intensive food, they were eating healthy; but it would be a shame to let them go bad, so maybe just one?

First come first served, and after a while I waited for the first person to open the box and strike empty, but it never came. About two dozen people had thanked me before I did the math and began to wonder how many doughnuts were in a Draupnir dozen. When I lifted the lid, there was only one left.

As three of my team leaders came in with problems, I began to deal with the first, while the second and third could fight for the last doughnut. As I finished with the first problem, I looked over to see which of the remaining team leaders had snagged the last doughnut. Oddly, both of them seemed to be chewing on one. Before I could investigate further, I was dealing with the next two problems. As I began to work on their problems, the first team lead went to the doughnut box and. . . pulled out another doughnut!

When they left, I opened the box and found one doughnut left still. There was something very weird about this Draupnir's Delicious Doughnuts.

Work went surprisingly well; everyone was in a good mood. I must have been thanked by half a hundred people for the doughnuts, and at least a half dozen of them pledged to do the same next week. I only bought the one dozen; I just don't understand how there always seems to be one left.

At the end of the day, I took the last doughnut, and broke it into nine pieces. As was my practice on days when I felt the need to offer,

I cast the my offering to the ravens that perched in our parking lot, and asked them to take this offering for the Æsir, and Odin, lord of hospitality, for the blessings that his teachings about hospitality bring to our daily lives.

On the way home, I drove past where Draupnir's Delicious Doughnuts was, but the building is just not there. I have no idea how it came to just be there one Wednesday, and then gone forever. If you ever see their sign, I suggest you pull in and ask for a Draupnir Special. Those little golden rings bring endless joy for all. Keep your eye out for their sign: Draupnir's Delicious Doughnuts.

Highway of Heroes

Sacrifice is a topic that has many forms as it does connotations. There is what is offered as a gift of material, and that which is offered as a service. Often we make a small symbolic offering in physical form to remember a far greater non-material sacrifice. When the gods gave to us their understanding of duty, our undertaking those obligations became an offering, became a sacrifice and sacrament to them. While all know Odin the Victory Father as a god of war, our gods have as many reasons to serve as they have ways to honour service.

Tyr is the god of justice, the god of social order, and the price paid to keep it. Tyr gave up his sword arm in the binding of Fenris Wolf as proof that his honour mattered more than his power; thus symbolically sublimating the wolf of war to the needs of the people. He wears his scar proudly, made more rather than less by his offering.

Freya is remembered by modern pagans mostly as the goddess of love, and more trivially as the sower of strife to bring conflict. In fact she is remembered as receiving half, and indeed first pick of the valiant dead to her own hall, with the leavings going to Valhalla.

When we gather to remember the sacrifice of our fallen, when we pay tribute with praise and tears to those who offered their life's blood in our service, what chance is there that such actions are not witnessed by our gods? When they walk among us to see if we remember to honour such sacrifice, what face do we show them, and what face do they show us in return?

There is a stretch of Highway 401 that leads from CFB Trenton that has been renamed the Highway of Heroes. It is this route that the flag draped coffins of fallen Canadian Forces soldiers travel upon their return from Afghanistan and other war-torn lands. Families, old comrades, and grateful citizens line the overpasses when it is announced our dead return. Each of those who come out strives to pay homage to the Einherjar, the valiant dead. There are those among us who remember how, and the teachers who once taught our ancestors walk among us still, instructing those with the will but not the words.

He was a young man, fit and hard, in his prime. The ghastly wounds that turned his eyeless face into a testament of pain did not touch his lips, which bore a sad smile, and grim determination. He was dressed with painstaking care, almost military precision, from his white shirt and regimental tie to his black suit and mirror-shined shoes. Defiantly, he smoothed out the dark green beret, with its crowned star of the RCR (Royal Canadian Regiment). Unsnapping a white cane as he moved away from the bus stop, he tapped his way through the crowd and towards the overpass where the convoy of the fallen would pass.

Recent roadwork had made the overpass sidewalks broken and uneven, and the blind former solider moved with caution. A large man with an eagle's gaze saw the soldier's halting approach, and gestured to his fair companion. With a smile, she tucked her tawny furred gloves beneath her belt and moved to the soldier's side.

"Hello," she greeted him, with a smile so warm his sightless face could feel it. As she addressed him, the crowd parted before her as waves before a ship, enabling her and her companion to join the soldier as he searched for the way to the summit.

"Did you know the fallen?" the regal blonde asked, with a voice like warm honey.

"No" replied the young man, "They were 3rd Battalion, and I was second. But they were of my Regiment, they were brothers."

The older man growled a wordless agreement and moved to assist the soldier over the broken ground.

"Take my arm," the older man said, "the ground is treacherous."

The proud scarred soldier began to protest that he was not a cripple needing help, when the old man's iron left hand closed the blind soldier's own left hand on the scarred stump that remained of the old man's right arm. Rather than a smooth prosthetic, he wore nothing over his stump but its own scars. As the soldier felt the battle-scars on the old man's arm, he knew he was receiving aid, and not pity, from one who understood.

"Soldiers look after their own" spoke the old man, with a voice that rang like swords clashing, or a main gun round slamming into a tank breach. The two men nodded unconsciously, synchronously, as they acknowledged this most ancient truth.

The day was cold and drizzling, in the way of an Ontario fall, and the crowd huddled awaiting the line of hearses that brought back the fallen from the last storm of bloody fighting in the Sandbox. Reaching the railing at the overpass, the old man gently moved the young soldier's hand off his maimed right arm and onto the guard rail. The growing noise of the crowd and gentle clapping let the blind soldier know his brethren approached. Reaching into his gabardine pockets, he pulled out a beer. Cracking the beer, he raised it high and spoke:

"You stayed true to your oaths, true to your salt, true to your brothers. Your watch is done. "

Unknown to the blind man, the older man held out his arms like a drooping letter T and raised his eyes to the sky. His blonde companion opened her jacket, revealing the gold and amber necklace that threw back the growing light of the pale autumn day like so much fire. As the young man continued to speak, the sky above the highway shone with light, the clouds drew back as if in reverence, and the sun lit the path of the fallen with rainbow splendor.

"We all talked about what we would do when we got back, and what we wanted if we didn't make it back. We all dreamed of getting back to the world, hoisting a cold one, and swapping lies in the Junior ranks' mess." His smile turned sad as he slowly tipped the beer over to let it pour out upon the highway below.

"You didn't make it home to swap lies with the rest of us, so hear the truth." His voice grew hard as iron, trembling with power.

"You fell in honour, not in defeat. Those who killed you dared not face you, such was the fear you taught them. The ground you died on, your brothers held, and every one will tell the tale of how you died doing your duty without fear or worry, without hate, and without ever forgetting who you were."

The last of the beer spilled now upon the stones.

"For you, buddies. First and best to the fallen. You will be remembered."

Some in the crowd looked sideways at what the blind soldier did, but if the warm glance of the women did not ease their scowl to a smile, the piercing eagle gaze of the one-armed warrior snapped their heads around.

The young man looked embarrassed and turned to his two companions to explain. "That used to be called a blót; you know, an offering. Our ancestors used to remember their fallen that way. I guess they hoped they would share the next one in Valhalla, but at least we know we greeted them with one when they came home"

The woman responded with a purring interest.

"Is this something you still do?"

The boy missed the long lingering looks both his companions were giving him. He pulled out another beer from his other pocket, and cracked it open.

"The other thing the ancestors did was sumbel, or passing a beer around, toasting the gods, each other, swapping lies about what they did, and promises about what they were going to do, and maybe letting off a little steam about stuff they couldn't admit was getting to them at the time; you know, the close ones. That part the army never really forgot." Raising the opened beer towards his two companions, he proffered it towards the woman's soft voice.

"Would you join me?"

The woman took up the beer and with the sunlight reflecting back from her necklace like a second sun, she raised the beer to speak first, and then drink.

"The Æsir!" she cried as she raised the beer towards her one armed escort.

She passed the beer to her companion's good hand. He accepted with a little bow and replied, raising the can towards her.

"The Vanir," he spoke with a voice like the clearest trumpet, then drank a steady pull.

The blind soldier raised the bottle up one more time towards the highway of heroes and concluded: "The fallen," and finished the beer. As he tucked the empty back into his coat, he muttered quietly to himself.

"Only the best will know Valhalla, the rest of us just muddle along and try to make sure what they fell for doesn't get sold or forgotten with the best of us gone. Even a blind man can help stand that watch."

As the three made their way back down the broken overpass towards the event bus from the local Legion and handed the young soldier back onto it, his two companions appeared lost in thought.

Raising his half-arm in salute to the departing bus, the old warrior turned his eagle gaze onto the golden woman and asked with gentle humour, "Do you think he will find Valhalla?"

The woman's laugh was trilled like birdsong and brought a smile to the lips of passers-by. She pulled on her golden furred gloves and shot her companion a satisfied smile.

"I think he will find himself someplace far more agreeable."

His laughter sounded like a rolling thunder, and when it faded, so had they.

Offered And Taken

There are two ways that such sacrifices can be made. One can offer what is due, or one can wait until it is taken. Of the two, one is building a reciprocal gifting relationship, establishing and maintaining a positive balance with the spirits that share this world with us, and the second is letting your bills go to the universe's equivalent of collection. When your duties remain undone, the price the universe exacts for inattention to duty is often far more brutal and permanent than the cost, however high, would have been to take up our burden, and fulfill even the most difficult of our responsibilities.

Undertaken for the right reason, usually necessity on some level, the act of sacrifice is the most heathen of acts, for it brings a gift for a gift. Often times those gifts take long to recognize or appreciate, but others are more immediately noted. Tyr gave up his arm for his honour, Odin his eye for knowledge. Our gods bear the signs of their sacrifice without artifice or shame, proud of the scars of their offerings. In this there is a lesson. Sacrifice is not shameful. To have offered of yourself in a worthy cause is to have earned great worth: a thing of pride and not shame at all.

The boy was angry and proud, scared, and pretty sure he was screwing up. In that awkward angry phase between boy and man where all manner of stupid things seem inescapable, and looking like he wasn't going to live past it, Brennan knew what he had; his dad's old service pistol, his gang colours, and no hope.

Growing up in rural Newfoundland—known affectionately as the Rock to those lucky enough to leave—offered little but unemployment, poverty, and the choice between getting out or giving up. Thrown into the mix were a surprising number of immigrants who had largely taken advantage of Gander's status as the Soviets' only non-Communist stopover to Cuba to defect, and the usual Third World exiles who jumped ship from the heavy freighter traffic of the East Coast, and you had an explosive mix for angry youths.

Brennan had grown up raised by his grandmother, as his mother had not borne up well when his father was killed on deployment overseas. Her stories of the old country had resonated with the ancient-seeming land called Newfoundland by the Scots, French and Scandinavians who settled her, but had failed to hold his interest when he ran into trouble in school. Finding a home with a group of would-be skinheads, Brennan and his friends learned there was strength in numbers, and status in being feared. It all seemed so cool until things got out of hand. One fight led to a stabbing, and the word came down: payback was owed. Doug told Brennan he was ready to become his number one. All he had to do was take his father's gun and get a little payback.

"Stupid, stupid, stupid, effing stupid" he cursed as he stomped through the woods to the old lake. No one ever came here; the lake was cold, small, and had a reputation for drowning people. His grandmother used to tell him stories about sea hags, and how they would snatch sailors from the ships and drag them down into the deeps when men forgot to ask for what they took from the sea; she thought one might have been storm-carried into the loch years ago. He used to come here to party with the Lords (his crew), until Jason got too stoned and drowned in the lake. Now he came here to think.

He can't go back and face the Lords without getting payback, or he would be a punk to them, worse than nothing. He couldn't go back and kill somebody, just because two guys got mad and got into it. He was screwed either way. He clutched at his dad's gun; it was the only answer he had, even if it was a bad one. It was kind of pathetic: his father the peace-keeper left it to protect his family. Now Brennan was going to use it to spark a gang war.

He looked at the old dock where Jason drowned. They used to hop from pole to pole to get to the broken dock, but Jason must have been too stoned to make it, or the slimy poles were just too treacherous. Brennan had the courage of the lost, and grimly hopped out to the broken dock just like they used to when it all still made sense. He was so lost in thought, he never heard the old woman come, or saw her boat. There was no way someone who looked like his grandma's grandma jumped over, and her shapeless green dress was bone dry.

"I know that look, boy. That's the feuding look. Some of the first ones had that, when they come here getting away from a bad one in the old country. The Highlanders, they brought it with them when they came too." She cackled a harsh crow cackle.

"Blood calls for blood, and never enough."

"Pride, boy, it's always been worth dying for. Gods know it's little comfort living for."

Brennan grew angry, women never understood. It was something only men understood. "My father lived his pride, he was a soldier."

Brennan felt a smack like a tree branch clap him hard against the back of his head; the old woman's hand was harder than a tree root, and colder than the half frozen pier.

"Your father lived his honour, and made your mother proud." The old woman muttered to herself, but Brennan listened:

"Honour serves others, bringing peace and earning worth. Pride serves itself, bringing strife, and leaving filth. I take my price either way, so I should not care. But honour shines in my memory, blood and foolishness brings only shame."

Brennan looked at the gun at his belt, and the swastika burned into his jean jacket, the symbol of the Lords. His father would hardly be proud of that, and there was no honour in killing some random kid just for "payback" that would only lead to more blood, more pain. He looked at the waters that took Jason, and told the old woman:

"I lost a buddy here, last springtime. Jason. He wouldn't have hesitated, he would have got payback already. It's a shame he died here. They say the lake takes a life every year, even it doesn't seem to care about killing people at random, why should I!" He was nearly shouting at the end, with tears standing unshed in his eyes.

The old woman turned her dark green eyes upon Brennan and spoke clear and cold as the winter's ice. "The lake always gets a life. Sometimes it is offered, sometimes it is taken, but she always gets her due." She poked the swastika on the jacket, muttering, "Sun wheel, hey? Not a lot of sunshine in anybody wearing it these days. Nothing but darkness, anger and shame." Looking Brennan in the eye she tapped the gun and swastika and demanded:

"Is that your life? Killing because you're too proud to admit you're making a mistake? Or are you going to try for honour instead? It's a harder life boy, but cleaner."

Brennan looked at his father's gun, and knew he couldn't murder with it. With a sigh he let it slip into the water. "A present for you Jason, you would have dug it." He had no idea what he was going to do. He was not going to let a war start, though. He remembered Jason dying, and was not going to get used to funerals because everyone was too proud and stupid to stop. He'd stop them himself. Maybe that was just as stupid, but honour stupid, not pride stupid. At least it might make his mother proud he fell keeping the peace just like his

19

dad. Decision made, he tossed his "colours" into the water too, the last ties to his old life.

The sun was going down, and he had to get home, so he bid the old woman good bye and jumped for the first pole back to shore. So long sitting in the cold had left him stiff, and he just about fell off the pilling and into the freezing water. Just as he started to slip, an iron hard claw grabbed him by the arm and slung him up onto the pier. Without seeming to move, the old woman had covered the distance between them in a heartbeat, and handled his weight like nothing.

"You already offered one life here," she said kindly. "That is so much worthier than one taken."

When Brennan jumped the last pole back to shore and looked back, the old woman was gone, like she slipped into the black water or something. He had no idea if this new life was going to last beyond telling Doug and the Lords that payback was stupid, and he wasn't doing it. That was OK; if he had to choose between killing some innocent person, or getting hit by his own guys, at least he would die clean. The old woman was right about that too, even with his own life: it was worth so much more when offered freely trying to do the right thing, than taken randomly because he started a gang war.

The lake is still watching, silent and patient. They say it takes a life every year, but Brennan always corrects them. The lake receives a life every year. Sometimes it is offered freely, others it is taken.

Cats-paw

The act of sacrifice has power. There have always been, and will always be, those who understand the power of sacrifice as well as its price, and who have determined the most cost effective way of getting what they want is to let others pay the price.

This is the truth of politics and economics on many levels, as time and again humanity pays the price to learn, and relearn the ancient truth that there really is no such thing as a free lunch. In 1966's The Moon is a Harsh Mistress, Robert Heinlein popularized the TANSTAAFL principle: There Ain't No Such Thing As A Free Lunch. The enduring belief that we can get something for nothing, or let others pay the price for what we desire without any personal consequence, has contributed much to the tragic history and ongoing foolishness of our species.

To make a sacrifice, one must consider three things to be successful. Consider whom it is you are sacrificing to. Consider what it is you are offering. Consider what it is you are seeking inside the context of whom you are offering to, and what it is you are offering. The act of sacrifice will get the attention of the gods, wights and ancestors. Unfortunately attracting their attention is only a good thing if your answers to the first three questions stand up to scrutiny. Ambition and honest self-awareness are often at odds, which also contributes both to the comedy and tragedy of human history. Mostly the latter.

Renowned to modern folk primarily as a goddess of love, Freya was known to our ancestors as a mercurial being of great power, foremost among all magicians. With her catskin gloves and knowledge equaled only by Odin, she was a figure of both wonder and terror. Beautiful and terrible were once commonly accepted together, even if modern man seems to have forgotten that we told fairy tales around the fire at night as we huddled in the light, glancing and shuddering at the fearful shadows.

Lisa was a bright and studious girl, who was just established in her own apartment for the first time. A junior at University of Victoria (UVic), she rented a room at an old house just off campus that was subdivided to make six mini apartments for students. They shared a kitchen and untidy communal living room, but her room had space enough for a desk, bed, bookshelf, mini-fridge, and litter-box for Amber.

Amber was Lisa's cat; while he was the family's cat in theory, he had lived in Lisa's room, been cared for, and walked (you can walk a cat if you are determined enough), by Lisa every day, and when Lisa left home, Amber and Lisa simply accepted it as a fact that they would leave together, and so it was.

On the corner of Lisa's desk was a small altar and offering bowl. Every day she would pour out a measure from her first coffee to Freya, goddess of magic, passion, and, she had decided, the patron of those seeking degrees in education (teaching=herding cats). She also left offerings at the battered garden gnome at the front door, for the house wights. She was pretty sure that Aiko (the Japanese girl) was doing the same.

Friday morning she got dressed, threw on a hoodie (UVic Vikings) against the fall chill, and snapped on Amber's leash. Off to the local Bolshevik Bean, with its tattered red star and fading Che Guevara poster, she ordered her weekend treat of breakfast wrap and Pumpkin Spice latte with extra whip. Amber patiently awaited his share of the whipped cream, while rumbling a happy approval at the all-organic actual whipped cream the hippy owners insisted on. Across the café, one brooding boy observed the girl and cat with a smile that had much more cat-cruelty than anything human.

He was not young, unlike the bulk of the clientele being neither student nor staff of UVic, but a worker at the local video game store. He wore a Satanic T-shirt and inverted pentacle, bore a sloppy mixture of tattoos of various arcana from Celtic to Egyptian, and wore a short goatee and fierce glare that clearly intended to shock or challenge. This effect was clearly lost on a crowd of busy college students who hailed from a number of faiths and ideologies whose happy clash was the norm for the University and faded into the background, unnoticed.

His name was Greg, but he had begun to go by Stavros, because he felt that was far cooler and was truer to his own nature, which he felt was dark and powerful. Through years of social rejection from peers that didn't get his interests, he had decided he was deeper than other people, and when his fascination with the dark, with atrocities and need to continually shock others caused those in the gaming communities to reject him, he turned to magic. He had tried the local pagan communities, and even the local Satanists, and all had rejected

22

him. They were afraid, all of them, like that little bourgeois feeding her cat across the way. She was pretty, but wouldn't look at him twice. He sneered; he decided he had a use for her, and her cat would help him get it. Laughing, he finished his coffee and waited for her to leave. He would follow to see where she lived.

Leaving a small piece of her morning wrap at the garden gnome, for the house wights, Lisa traded cat for laptop and binder, scratched Amber behind the ears, and asked her to guard the place for her until she returned. As she left Amber bathing himself in the window, she noted the "creepy guy" from the game store was on the sidewalk out front. Funny, she had never come this way before. Thinking little of it, she ran to catch the bus into campus.

Stavros waited until the little student bourgeois all left for the drone academy, and went to the old window that the cat was in. Knowing the old houses, he used his belt knife to push the lock on the window open, then forced it open. The cat hissed and backed away. Having heavy work gloves on, he grabbed the cat, and stuffed him into the gym bag, and zipped it quickly up. Now he had what he needed for the full moon tonight. A little bit of blood, and he would get for himself the fear and respect he deserved! These bourgeois children knew nothing about real power. . .

When Lisa got home it was almost dark, and her room was bitterly cold. Her room had been robbed! Her iPod and charger were still there, her electronics were all there; only her altar had been disturbed, as if Amber had retreated to it, and been taken from it. Her Freya statue was broken, and her offering bowl was chipped. Amber was gone! Who would steal a cat, when the SPCA had so many? Anyone who would give a good home to a cat could get one, so why break in and steal it?

The police were little help. With nothing stolen, and with no known enemies to question, the only thing they could do was give her a complaint number and add to her fears. Before they left, the police told her that some "sick freaks" liked to kill cats as part of that "black magic and shit"—they said, while pointing at her little altar. Too shocked to be insulted by the police implications that her Freya altar was black magic, she suddenly had the fear that someone might have taken Amber for the purpose of hurting him. There were, after all, people the SPCA would NOT give a cat to after all.

The whole house having searched the neighborhood, and put posters up of Amber on the nearby telephone poles, Lisa returned home dejected and scared. Amber was gone, and there was nothing she could do. She stopped at Bolshevik Bean to get her nightly pumpkin spice, but hadn't the heart to drink it without Amber. She stopped at the garden gnome on the way into the house, and poured the whole coffee and whip onto the stones. She looked up into the night sky, at the rising full moon and asked Mani the moon to watch over her cat, Amber, then she begged Freya to see that Amber got home safely. Normally Lisa was careful not to do magic, or curses, or to ask the gods for anything that could harm another person, as she was very uncomfortable with how her father and his army friends were so quick to see violence as an answer; but the thought of Amber being taken to be hurt angered her. She concluded her prayer thus: "Great Freya, if anyone sheds one drop of my Amber's blood, I hope they frigging die!"

Lisa went inside to cry herself to sleep. Outside in the night, three neighborhood cats came to lick the foam from the gnome's offering bowl, and the moon shone down white and cold above the now empty bowl.

Stavros didn't like research. It was way too much work pawing through boring book after book, either by archeologists who didn't believe anything, or by fuzzy brained pagans or stoned loser Satanists who believed everything. He watched a couple of horror movies that really struck him, though, and through his gaming had found gods that promised power, the kind of power that would make him feared by all the little people who thought it was safe to laugh at him.

There was a big mausoleum in the cemetery. He knew that the graveyard was the right place to do the spell at full moon because that's the way they did it in the film. There was one mausoleum that looked like a great granite table, supported by four carved stone pillars. Inside were the remains of a few generations of families, but in the moonlight it looked like a black stone altar. He set his candles at four corners, and spray-painted his pentagram on the altar. He had written out the spells from the movie: three hieroglyphs that were supposed to inspire fear in men that saw him, lust in women that saw him, and bring him victory over his enemies. According to the movie, you had to draw them in the blood of your victim first, then kill him to make it happen. Of course in the movie, the heroes stopped the priest while he was doing some stupid chanting and praying, so Stavros was just going to do this fast, and get out before a security guard or cop showed up.

Pulling the cat out of the bag, Stavros almost lost the little thing, as it clawed and scratched at him, even through the gloves. Slamming it down against the altar so hard it was stunned, he cut it with the knife he laid beside the altar, and started to paint the symbols on the surface of the stone. It was hard with the cat writhing, and the candle and moonlight shifting, and the need to speak his spell at the same time.

"Set, god of darkness, by this blood—stop it you stupid cat—I summon you. Fear in men, lust in women, victory and power I call!"

A woman's laughter seemed to come from all around, and the little cat went very still. The moonlight burned clear of the clouds, and Stavros stood in a pool of white fire as the shadows drew back from him. Blinded by the light, the knife gleaming wetly in his gloved hand, Stavros paused as he heard the woman's laughter getting closer. Set wasn't a chick, was he?

Four glowing gold eyes gleamed in the darkness. Alternating between high and low as they seemed to flow seamlessly and soundlessly over the coffins and headstones, they were wide set, like large dogs, but slit like snakes' or cats' eyes. A deep rumbling joined the night, like the growl of jungle cats.

"Fear, little man, I give to you. Lust, little man, I will share with you. Victory, little man, I will work on you."

A woman strode through the graves with languid prowl, as much like a cat as a dancer. A necklace of amber and gold flashed from her ample cleavage, and her hair caught the moonlight like the sunset's own fire. On her hands were gloves of soft fur, like catskin.

Left and right, on the headstones leaped great golden cougars. Their ears flat, their fangs gleaming wide and white in the moonlight, their throaty growls now turned his blood to water, and loosed his bladder down his leather pants.

"That is fear, little man. That is first. This cat is not yours, little man. He is mine, and another's. Tree-Gold and Bee-Gold here are mine as well"—she gestured languidly at the mountain lions whose tails lashed in blood hunger and hunt-lust. "One who also owns this cat had offered me your life's blood, should you draw Amber's blood. Your knife is as stained as your pants, little man."

She laughed again with the casual cruelty of a cat, and with a throaty purr continued:

"Your life is mine. Run swift, sweetling, my children like to play with their food. If they don't get a good run first, they take their time with the finish."

Stavros ran screaming, but in the darkness, the graves themselves tripped him up, and he fell again and again, each time being savaged by one or the other cat, until at last he was slow to rise, and Bee-gold took the killing neck bite.

Cooing softly, the golden woman took up the wounded cat. "Little Amber, let mother see to you." Moonlight flashed like so much fire upon her necklace, calling sun-colour to moon-dark, until it seemed that gold ran down the woman's arms onto the bruised and bloodied cat.

As Stavros's screams turned to broken moans, the cooing of the woman began to be answered by purrs of the little cat, as if his wounds themselves burned away in her light. Setting him down, they walked together to the broken man upon whom the two mountain lions were feeding. With the aplomb of any cat, he shouldered his way between their two great heads, and lapped delicately at the life-wine spilling from his throat. Sharing an amused look, the twin lions returned to their mistress to leave their cousin to his revenge repast.

The woman looked up at the bright moon in the sky and said, "I expect you to see him home again. My little friends are less welcome on the streets."

Lisa woke the next morning shivering in the cold. In the night her window had opened again, and her beloved Amber was curled up on the bedspread behind her knees. As she took up her beloved pet in wonder, her eyes caught her altar, where her broken Freya statue was somehow restored. Looking upon the blood her cat was happily and smugly licking off herself, and remembering her evening prayer, she wondered. . .

Chapter 2: Loss, and Change

Endings

How central to our existence is change? Yet how feared. Life is change, with the final change being death. There is wonder and horror, fear and joy in equal measure. There are times when one side of the coin is obvious, and the other hard to see, but both are always present.

To love is to give a hostage to fortune, to dare is to invite failure, to have it to face loss. We cannot run from the negatives by failing to embrace the positives. We cannot outrun death, but we can, and too many do, miss much of the joy and worth in life by trying. Dealing with loss, with change, and with death is something we all must face, and we are seldom as alone as we think. At those moments when we can't see any options at all, when we see only the death of what was, and not the birth of what will be, listen carefully, and you will hear the whisper of your gods and ancestors offering a nudge forward. Every once in a while they step beyond the shadows to nudge us more directly.

One of the problems we have as modern as modern people is accepting the truths our ancestors, without our medical technology, our wealth, or even our birth control, had no choice but to face early and often. To love was to lose. To live was to embrace death as a constant, but to love all the more fiercely while you could. The goddesses associated with motherhood and the hearth, like Mother Frigga, are darker than most modern people would expect a mother goddess to be, because to be a mother meant embracing necessity as the cost of survival. The pain of life is given to you, the loss in life comes to you. To know joy, hope, or love you must embrace the cost, accept the change, and dare to risk again. Mothers can be harder than stone, for sometimes we must be forced from the nest, forced into the pain we would avoid, if we are to know the joy of flight or the embrace of life again.

She had come to the pier with a stolen bottle of vodka, and her own bottle of pills. Fourteen years was enough. It was time to end things. The pier itself was dark, and the walkway down to the floating dock was treacherous; cold metal slick with evening damp and river mist. No druggies, young lovers, or fishermen waited below. It was dark and silent, save for the remorseless lapping of the dark waters of the Fraser.

No one understood her rage, her pain, her fear. Life was a trap, a cold dark box that pressed closer and closer, pushing at her until the walls left her no room to do anything but pound the walls and scream. They wouldn't let her change schools, although, since her friends at other schools from dance had heard all about her troubles, probably everyone on Facebook, Twitter, or Instagram knew every humiliating detail of her life. There was no place to run once everyone was against you, and no way out except one.

There were times in the past that she would come down here with her family, to make offerings to the gods her father talked about, and she rejected. She turned to her Grandmother's God to ask forgiveness, to get him to take her pain away, and make it all better. She went to church, she said the words, she begged, she prayed, she waited, but her problems didn't. For all her prayers, for all her tears, and rage and screaming, her problems ground on like some uncaring glacier, tearing her life like the bones of the mountain pass, ground to nothing beneath the uncaring ice. She opened the cap of the vodka and took a gulp, coughing as the white fire burned and her stomach flinched against its fury.

"Not a good sign drinking alone," said the voice of an old woman, sitting unnoticed beneath the ramp of the pier. "Even worse drinking angry in the dark," the iron voice of the crone continued. "Gives a body all kinds of bad ideas."

Kate whipped around, her trademark fury only ever a heartbeat from the surface. She began to scream a demand the woman show herself, but her shout died as she turned and stared into the cold milky white eyes of the blind woman sitting on the pier. Her eyes were blue once, but covered now with a web of white cataracts. Her once blonde hair hung in a single neat rope of silver and gold, as she sat unravelling the half-knit sweater in her hands. Her face was strong and open; lines of laughter, pain, fear, loss, and love radiated from her eyes, while her brow and chin promised uncompromising resolve. This was a timeworn face, one that had outlived its fears, embraced its pain, and had all weakness ground away in the tide of years.

"You would be Kate," the old woman said simply. "You can call me Oma."

Kate finally stammered a response, her anger dashed on Oma's calm sightless eyes. "What are you doing here?" she finally asked.

Oma held up the sweater, and yanked hard on the trailing yarn to unravel a row.

"Unmaking, ending, sundering" she chanted, each word a yank on the yarn. "Fabric is like family, every thread bound to every other, and a single weak one can ruin the lot."

Kate rocked back on her heels as if slapped, and tears burned in her eyes, spilling down her cheeks. They were there for the same purpose. Ending of threads, cutting out the unwanted.

"Are you drinking alone, or would you share with an old woman whose bones feel the cold more than they did at your age, girl?" Oma asked gruffly.

Wordless, she handed the bottle over and the old woman moved to pour it over the flowing river. Her mouth open to object, for she thought the old woman was dumping out her hard-stolen bottle. She saw, instead, the old woman pour out two small measures, as her parents sometimes did when they offered to the false gods her father talked about.

"Wights of this place for welcoming us," she poured once. A pause, then again: "To my poor dead children, I carried you with love, bore you in pain, and buried you too soon. A mother remembers, forever."

"Your children are dead?" Kate asked with a halting voice

"Two in the mound, including my first. Some still live, and grandchildren too. Life goes on, even in times we can't imagine why it should."

"What about your husband?"

"Hah!" the old woman barked. "Look for him at the cenotaph, the old wolf's name is written on there if you have eyes to see it. Of course, he only had the one, and it wandered enough when pretty little things like you were around. But he kept me warm at night, and made me laugh."

The old woman handed the bottle back, and turned to her knitting. "This thread was weak, and when I knitted on it failed. Now I have to go back and cut it out."

Kate's cheeks burned in shame, and she took a second pull on the bottle, and muttered agreement. "No use for weak threads in this world, you may as well just cut them off before they wreck everything."

Oma laughed, her voice suddenly warm and soft, like the feel of sunshine, or a mother's kiss. "They are all weak threads, child," the old woman said gently.

With a quick twist she knotted the broken yarn and took up her needles. As the soft clicking of the needles and the lapping of the waves worked with the lapping of the waves to lull the crying teen into a daze.

"Families are like this sweater, made of imperfect threads born in one place, died in another, touching each other a thousand times a thousand ways, each pulling on each other across the whole of the sweater. Even if a dozen breaks are between them, the line is unbroken. Families are like this sweater, maybe not so bright and perfect as you see on the shelf, but grown strong in the broken places, warm and comforting, with each thread together stronger than any could be alone."

Kate's eyes grew strangely heavy as she slumped to the ground, all strength fading with the dregs of her rage. She sat quietly with the tears streaming freely.

"Sit with Oma-Frig, little Kate," the old woman said. "Keep me company, for my children are long gone from my hearth, and it has been too long since anyone fell asleep on my lap."

Too proud to speak to anyone about what was hurting inside her, and too proud to accept help when it was offered, Kate was half woman-to-be that must stand alone, and half child-that-was needing to be held. Nothing to prove to sightless eyes, she curled up beside Oma-Frig, placed her head on her lap, and wept silently.

She fell asleep listening to the lapping of the waves, the clicking of the needles and a lullabye sung is a language she did not know. Hours later, she woke up to the old woman drying her eyes, and wrapping her in the warm cable-knit fisherman's sweater.

"Here child, to your own hearth you best be getting, before folks get worried enough to ask questions you don't need to be answering." The old woman laughed gently. "Since I've gone and finished that little bottle to keep me warm, I will leave you this sweater to keep you warm in turn. A gift for a gift is the way."

As Kate walked back up the pier, she felt along the sweater looking for the broken thread. The blind woman must have heard her hands sliding along the wool for she called out to Kate:

"If you are looking for the broken place child, you won't find it. Sweaters are like families, they grow stronger in the broken places. We are all weak threads child, knotted and tangled, torn and broken."

She rammed her needles into the yarn like a swordsman sheathing a blade.

"You tie off at the break, and knit on."

Feeling her way to the guardrail with Kate's help, Oma continued. "No matter how far apart the threads have grown, time will pull them tight again, and the rough spots are what gives the pattern form. When you have been knitting as long as I have, you trust the weave. Even your two good eyes can't see what hasn't been woven yet."

Kate turned towards home, as the old weaver, Oma, turned the other way. When she turned to say goodbye, the old woman was gone. Hugging the sweater tight, Kate made her way back home. None of her problems were gone, the tangle was still a tangle, and she still saw no way out. Sometimes you just have to trust the weave, and learn to grow strong in the broken places.

Helm of Awe-some

Loss is something that humanity as a species should be used to, for we begin our instruction with the loss of the womb, and continue right through to the loss of our life. Having said that, dealing with loss is something we often struggle with, and sometimes give up too many opportunities simply to avoid.

There are many ways of dealing with loss, some are healthy, and some are workable; some are costly and damaging. There are as many ways of dealing with loss as there are people and losses to deal with. Some people respond well to what are traditionally viewed as the acceptable and healthy choices. Others do not value the same things in their life, and thus will not respond to loss in the same way. To be successful at dealing with loss, you must be true to yourself, and put it always in terms of what is important to you, rather than what is expected to be important to you.

Viðar Jawbreaker, called the silent one, is a god that once received the offerings of boot makers, as it was his boot that opened the jaws of the dread wolf at Ragnarok to avenge Odin. The silent one, the vengeful one; so he is remembered. Yet his offering were those of a builder, a doer. His ways were not words, but deeds, practical rather than poetic. What sort of wisdom might such a god have for those who live in a world such as ours?

Judy was 14 and active. She had been in soccer since she could remember, and lived as much of her life outdoors as she could, never happier than when on her skateboard or snowboard. It wasn't that she was obsessed with doing the big tricks and aerials, it was just she learned from the day she could walk that she was going to spend the majority of her life going from point a to point b and it was either going to be sitting in a box waiting, or out in the world living.

Grandpa Jim was always saying "Time enough for sitting in a box when you're dead. Stuff to do, stuff to do!" He was a crazy old fart, but right. Life was what you were missing sitting in a box, and what she was doing on her board in the bike lane of King Edward on her way back from soccer. In the lane beside her was a man in a box. His box was a Dodge Ram with a lift kit and big shiny truck nuts hanging from the rear of an immaculately detailed truck that knew far more valet parking than mud. He had a cell phone tucked between his shoulder and neck, and was trying to jot down a sales appointment in his book while he raced the lights at King Edward.

The Smart Car in front noted that the light just switched to red, and coasted to a stop. Judy had been standing tall, also coasting to a stop, as any idiot could see the light was going to be red long before she got there. Mr Busy glanced up from his appointment book to see the smart car stopped dead in front of him, and rammed the wheel hard over while standing on the brakes. One ton of hurry ground Judy's left ankle into fragments of bone and blood on the uncaring stone.

Tears were in her eyes, and she was shaking with shock, but not a sound came from her. Her board helmet had crushed when she hit the ground, saving her skull. She managed to get her phone out and call 911 before passing out. She could hear the loser in the truck screaming at the woman in the Smart Car. I guess that was more important than some girl in the gutter.

Waking in hospital was not fun. She got told she was losing the foot, but she could see what they were doing, they meant the lower leg. Soccer was gone, boarding was gone. Her life was gone. Rage filled her before the sedatives took her. She went down into the dark, unwilling to return. The doctors showed more care than some drivers, and she returned, willing or not.

Judy had sat through a thousand lectures in her bed about how "It's not her fault but..." Her family made it quite clear that boarding was the problem. They brought her helmet to show her how dangerous her choices were, and she clutched it with a grim ferocity and snarling that drove them back. What they saw as a lesson in how to stay safe, she saw as a lifeline, the last link to what made life worth living. They failed to agree, even to disagree. Judy decided she was a majority of one. Boxes were for dead people, you could only live in the world. If she couldn't live, she would rather be dead already.

He came on Wednesday. She had been dreading it. Once they strapped that fake foot on, you were a cripple for life. No more pretending it would get better. That was it. Existing rather than living for an eternity before she passed from the last safe box into the box she was buried in. Today they fit her for her new foot. Today she became a cripple.

Everyone was relentlessly cheerful, smiling, and judgmental. She loved her parents dearly, but honestly, if they put one more "but" after a statement of "not your fault" she was going to murder them. Not much chance of a getaway at the moment. Mom sent her Pastor in. One more word about "God's Plan" and she was sending him to meet the old fraud in person. Really, the false cheer was taking a bleak future and turning the grey into deepest black. Rage or tears, and if she started crying, she wouldn't stop, so rage it was.

Judy was sitting in bed staring out the window at kids boarding in the parking lot when something eclipsed the lights. She turned to see a huge biker or linebacker with a hospital ID tag and a box of gear you could probably hide a mastiff in with room for a pair of Dobermans. His face was grim, his lips a hard uncompromising line, his eyes cold grey that seemed to say they had seen it all before, and weren't impressed then either. His name tag said Vithar, an odd enough name—she couldn't say if it was first or last.

He tapped the sheets over her missing leg and grunted. It should have been rude, but after all the false cheer and strangers calling her honey, sweetie and dear, it was oddly welcome. She pulled off the sheets, and he examined the wound. His initial grunt and frown were replaced with a low granite-like rumble as he took a tape and took a few measurements. After a while he took the tape and measured one leg, and then the other, then frowned again.

"Used to have muscle on this, ja?" he barked. "Going to have muscle on it again, or going to stay off it? I have to match them." It didn't sound like he cared one way or the other.

She felt the rage bubble up, and for some reason, with this grim stranger she felt freer than with her relentlessly cheerful parents (granddad would have understood, but he was gone).

"What difference does it make, it's not like I can do anything!"

Vithar had either never heard of rhetorical questions, or didn't much care when they happened, because he reached into his bag and slammed two limbs on the bed between her legs. One was pale and perfect, an elegant ankle that would look at home on a model. The other was a solid brutal hunk of steel and plastic with a joint that looked like it belonged on motorcycle suspension, rather than a person.

He pointed to the one. "That pretty. Easy."

He pointed to the second. "That hard work me, hard work you, but maybe get back most what you lost. Not all though. I gave up miracles centuries ago. Never worth it."

35

Look like she was whole, or look like a cripple for the rest of her life. It seemed simple. A crow call caused her to look out the window and see the kids boarding in the parking lot. She fingered the odd ball joint of the steel joint, and gestured with her chin. Not daring to ask the question. He shrugged with a little smile that promised nothing but a chance.

With a snarl she kicked the pretty leg off the bed, tears streaming down her face. He chuckled, and tapped her leg like you would tap a favoured hound, packed up, and left.

In the days that followed, her parents, siblings, nurses and doctors all returned to their lectures. Vithar returned and fit the leg. It clunked down the hall like the Terminator, but she was learning to pivot on it, and working on lunges, getting her muscle back, learning to do more than walk like a little old person.

Vithar came back again to test the fit. She asked him how he got into this work. He thought about it.

"Uncle, he lost hand. Can't help. Don't do hands. Brother, he got rock in skull, can't help, don't do heads. Did boots, did feet. Can do this."

She had been listening to the lectures about never risking her life on a board again; listening, but not agreeing. She wanted to know Vithar's thoughts.

"Your uncle who lost the hand, did he change?"

Vithar looked grim, shook his head, with a snort that implied his uncle was unlikely to let something as paltry as the loss of limb change him.

"Your brother with the skull, did he change?"

Vithar laughed silently, and pointed to her crushed helmet. "Wife make him wear those now. I make." They both chuckled.

She took her place on the wobble board, a simple plank with an inflatable ball in the middle that forced you to shift your balance from side to side. Child's play to a boarder like herself, Olympic-level challenge for amputees with their first prosthetic. She worked and and worked at it. She sunk low, remembering the feel of the board and the road, but then fear took her, she remembered the crash, she went stiff, and lurched off the board.

Vithar stood silent and waited. Judy looked down at the ground, and kicked the wobble board as if just to remind herself it was there. She spoke to him the truth she never whispered to any of those who would keep her from her beloved boarding, from doing anything except locking herself up in a box for the rest of her life. "I get scared sometimes. I freeze sometimes. I don't want to do that; I don't want to be that. How do I get past it?"

Vithar smiled, an expression that made him look more like a wolf than a grandfather; but his words were welcome. "There was a time that men held other gods, other ways, other truths. They accepted death and pain and loss, it was just a part of life. They did not accept fear. Fear would get you killed, at best, or keep you from living at all, at worst. They spat on fear. They mocked it. They drove it off.

"There was a thing, made of runes. A Helm of Awe. They cut it or burned it into their foreheads, a powerful protection that said they could not be killed, could not be stopped, could not be harmed. It was strong magic. It was not death they stood off, for death comes with birth and is always with you. It held off fear. It was a challenge."

Her eyes looked up at his, the cold grey now burning like sun off drawn steel. His voice rumbled like Harley wide open, or a charging bear.

"Helm of Awe says—here I am, seizing every last drop of life from this world, and there is NOTHING you can do to stop me!"

They looked at each other, wide brown eyes and snarl meeting wide blue eyes and snarl. She understood.

They met one last time as she prepared to leave the hospital. She filled out the paperwork to lease the wobble board for her own rehab. As she worked the board one last time in her room, he reached into his massive bag and asked her offhand.

"Will you ride again soon you think?"

She jumped heavily off the board. With her artificial leg she slammed down on the edge of the wobble board, causing it to jump up against her leg like a skateboard would. She grinned challengingly at him.

Without a word, he reached in and pulled out a skateboard helmet in black, with a silver Helm of Awe shining from its brow.

Smiling shyly, she put it on, and met his eyes one last time.

"Helm of Awesome," she said.

Taking the leavings of his boot-making, Vithar took his leave with the silent nod he usually did. Somehow, his trust that she had things under control and didn't need him to make a big deal, actually made things easier to control. She had this. She would do this. Life was lived outside the box or you were already dead. When did we forget that? She didn't care. She remembered.

Fish and Fate

There are times when you must face the loss of the one thing you would have sworn you could not live without, when the center of your world is cut away. The loss of a loved one, the loss of a way of life, or any of the central pillars that we base our sense of identity around. Often times these things are only really knowable as the center of our world when they are taken from us.

How do we deal with such losses? How can you go on when all that you care about is lost? It is in the darkest times that the smallest of lights can lead you back. It is in the silence between sobs that a single word can turn you back towards life again. Our ancestors lived with loss far more intimately than we did, and through their efforts we do not have to lose as frequently and terribly as they do. While we give thanks we rarely need to endure as they did, we also look to them for guidance when we too must face the loss our heart cannot bear. A broken heart still beats, our life is not over, and sometimes we need a little nudge to remind us.

Odin and Thor often wandered the worlds in mortal guise. Seldom did their coming foretell great events; most often it seemed they journeyed to see what humans did amongst themselves, to and for each other. The greatest gift the gods can give to us is not magic, is not shaking the earth or casting down cities; the greatest gift they can give to us is a word at the right moment, a nudge at the fork in the road.

She was gone in a heartbeat. Celeste had been the heart of his world, even if she was the only one that didn't know it yet. She had been his friend since college, his lover and roommate for the last two years, and he had intended to make her his fiancé when his position as engineer became formalized at work. She didn't care; she never needed anyone to look after her, determined to make her own way in the world, dependent on no one, even as she was always there for those who grew swiftly to depend upon her.

Then she was gone.

She had gone to bed with a headache, and it must have been a bad one because when he tucked a teddy bear he had bought her under her arm, instead of throwing it at him as she usually did, she clutched it to her breast, her pale and sweaty face showing the pain she was seeking sleep to escape. She did not wake. Cerebral hemorrhage. A cerebrovascular accident. Nothing that could have been seen, or treated, or stopped. Just one of those things.

But she was gone.

It was not enough. Charles was not good with rage, it was no part of his life, no part of his soul, but it was burning from his heart now, as the tears were from his eyes. How could he live without her? I mean, five years ago he didn't even know her, but somehow she had become the pillar of his world. Then she was gone, and his world was collapsing.

Celeste had been heathen, which was not Pagan. She had explained it about a thousand times, but he never really followed most of it. He had been to the events she hosted, and the ones she guested at, and the feasts were good, the people were straight-forward and down to earth. He had enjoyed being a part of her community even if he didn't understand it. He was an engineer; he believed in the universe his mathematics and models described. In his apprenticeship with the firm, he had begun to grasp the manifold ways the models failed to contain all reality, and the many ways the facts that were demonstrably true stood at odds with the most carefully constructed models. As Celeste was fond of quoting, "world-accepting" means accepting the things you can prove, even if you don't understand all of them. She could make even religion make sense. When she was with him, Sunna the sun shone down on them, bringing life to the ever renewing earth. Without her, a radioactive ball of gas blasted the earth with killing radiation that was imperfectly screened by atmosphere and magnetics as it spun in the uncaring and lifeless cold of the void. There was a difference.

He walked along the Port Mann bridge pedestrian tunnel. He had studied the bridge a lot when he was working on his bachelor's degree; his professor had done the design for the earthquake upgrades, and the stress studies on the bridge before and after had been part of his exam material. He never really looked at the river itself until Celeste took him. He brought her to show her the bridge, and in return she had introduced him to the river he had looked at a thousand times, and never seen, save as a chaotic force element in his stress diagrams.

She did that to his world, every place she went, she filled in blanks he never knew were there, lent colours to a world of cold lines and solids.

He stopped at the place the barrier had been taken down for the work crews. He looked out into the river, he took the half doughnut that she always had him bring and tossed it out on the water. The river carried it past, and he paid little attention to what took it. He didn't have the words, those were hers. He didn't even know why he bothered, except it would have pleased her.

He pounded the railing. Tears welled in his eyes. He hit again and again until his hand was bloodied, then gripped the railing and shook, too tired even to cry. He was shocked from his solitude and sorrow by a loud voice that sounded like it would be at home shouting over some high iron construction crew, or howling factory floor.

"Figure him for a jumper, Old Man?" The voice was more curious than concerned, but there was a warmth in it that suggested there was more likely to be sympathy than cruelty in its humour.

Charles turned to see two bearded fishermen; the one who spoke, a red-bearded giant of a man in an Iron Workers mackinaw. He glanced at the boy, then set about casting off the bridge with the snap of long practice. The heavy fishing rod looked like a child's plaything in his heavy paw, but the joy in his face as he watched the line sing out made him more of a childlike figure than a threat.

The Old Man in question was similar in size, but wrapped in a faded old battle dress jacket, worn shiny in the places where straps of webbing or pack would lie. Wild grey hair obscured half his face as he sized up the boy in a glance. Turning away, he flicked his own cast straight and true to the water below before making his ruling.

"No. Jumpers don't hurt themselves. They flee pain. This one hurts himself because the real pain he can't reach."

Charles went cold to see himself laid bare by this stranger's glance. His tone was cold and hard, like stone or steel, a simple statement of fact presented uncaring and unquestionable, not open to debate or doubt.

"What do you know about loss, old man!" Charles snarled, his wounds raw and weeping.

The red beard laughed, and cracked open the great stainless steel thermos, and began filling the cup with rich black coffee. He glanced at the boy, and tossed his head at the old man.

"That one, he knows more about death than most. More than he should, some say. Listen boy, you could do a lot worse." He handed

41

the steaming cup to the old man who locked his reel to the railing and raised high the cup.

"To my sons, my firstborn who fell to stupidity and mistake, my baby boys who grew up too fast, did a man's duty, and fell upon the field because they would let no other stand first into danger. To my daughter who loved perhaps more truly than wisely, and died of it."

He took a sip, and poured a splash to the swirling waters.

"To the fallen."

The redbeard took up the cup. "Roskva, you were a good woman, a wise and good guide to my children when my wife and I were caught up in things. You were always there, like the fire in the hearth that made our home bright, until the day age took you from us."

He took a sip, and poured out a splash unto the waves.

"Absent companions."

They handed the cup to him, and he took it in trembling hands. He raised it up as he remembered Celeste doing.

"To Celeste, you were my love, my friend, my world. I hoped we would have a chance to get married, have kids, grow old together. We didn't get that. You woke me up, showed me it's not enough to pass through life, you have to live it. Now I have to live it alone."

Tears burning his eyes, he took a sip of the coffee and choked, for it was over half rum. He spilled a little over the edge to the dark waters she had taught him to love.

"To those gone but not forgotten."

The cup passed in silence, with none needing more than the company of the others, and the solitude of their thoughts. Finally, in a voice weary, but no longer raging, Charles asked, "Celeste was always talking about wyrd, or fate. What the hell does that mean. Why did she have to die so young? She was so full of life, so full of joy, and she dies, while all these druggie losers, criminals, and scum live on!"

The old man said simply, "Fish."

Charles turned angrily and told them both in no uncertain terms what they could do with their fishing rods. Both men laughed, but the elder explained.

"FISH: F*ck it, Sh*t Happens. Wyrd weaves as it will, boy, there is no judgment to it. There is no cosmic purpose behind a brain aneurysm, or a drunk driver, or cancer, or a roadside bomb that took the truck behind you and not your own. Wyrd just is. We bury our dead, get back to life, and never let them be forgotten."

Charles sighed. It sounded like something Celeste would have said. If she had said it, it would have rung with wisdom and hope.

When the old man said it, it was simply cold fact, like the stress figures on a bridge arch. The figures just were. You either accepted them, and dealt with them, or nothing you built could last. It wasn't easy. But it was doable.

"Fish," he said, and drank deeply.

As the men walked to the end of the bridge, there was a big crew cab waiting for them, idling like a monster truck in the parking lot. They offered to drop Charles at his door. Charles thought himself familiar with all the construction firms in town, but didn't recognize the upside down hammer logo on the side. For that matter, the hood logo was screwed up too.

"Is it supposed to have two rams on the hood?"

The redbeard just laughed.

Claws in the Dark

There have always been things in this world that no strength of arm, no strategy or tactic of mind, no training or discipline will serve you against, before which our wealth of gold and knowledge mean nothing. It is against such silent, faceless enemies that we learn dark truths about ourselves and our limitations. Disease, whether genetic condition, infection, or malfunction (like cancer) is something that must be fought, but mostly by others. This is a battle in which the attacks belong to your medical team, but in which victory, while not always even possible, can only come through your simple brute endurance. Like a roof beam in a fire, all you can do is hang screaming or silent, and endure the burning until others have put out the fire, or you are consumed utterly.

For those who have endured such struggles, they will know how important motivation is, and how a positive attitude can help carry you through much of the struggle. There are limits to all things, to all strengths, and even to hope. When the last of the light fades, you have two choices, you may go down quietly into that final dark, or you may turn and make the acquaintance of the darkness within yourself, and take up the battle with tools forged not of love and hope, but with hate and rage.

Of light and dark are all men made, and light and dark are the natures of the wights of this good earth. Both light and svartly alf received offering from our folk. The wights of field and farm whose favour and company we sought received gifts from our ancestors when we invited them to join with us. The darker wights, the powerful and angry ones, received offerings as well, for while we did not invite them in, we acknowledged and offered to them as well, for our ancestors lived too close to the edge of survival to turn their backs on an ally whose aid may be what stands between them and loss, even if that ally was dark indeed.

It is in the times when the light fades, when hope dies, that you learn the truth about the darkness in yourself. If you have that self-honesty, that world-acceptance, the wights of the dark may aid you as well in turning your inner darkness to worthy ends, because it will always be inside you.

The choice is simply will you acknowledge, accept and harness it, or deny both its existence and your chance to control it?

Winterfinding had passed, and with it the light. Jasmin (Jay) felt like the world was mirroring her life. She had been a dancer, a field hockey player for her school. Now she was a "victim". She had cancer, and while it waxed strong in her, she waned.

Her mother and father were trying to be supportive, even her sister was, but she wasn't the girl she had been, the girl they needed her to be. Not all the time. Rage was new to Jay, hate was new. Despair was new, even if fear wasn't. The love and the light that was offered to her was important, she depended on it for strength, but sometimes when her strength was gone, when the light failed, there was something else in her, something bitter as gall, dark and cold. It was new, but it was hers, and it hated.

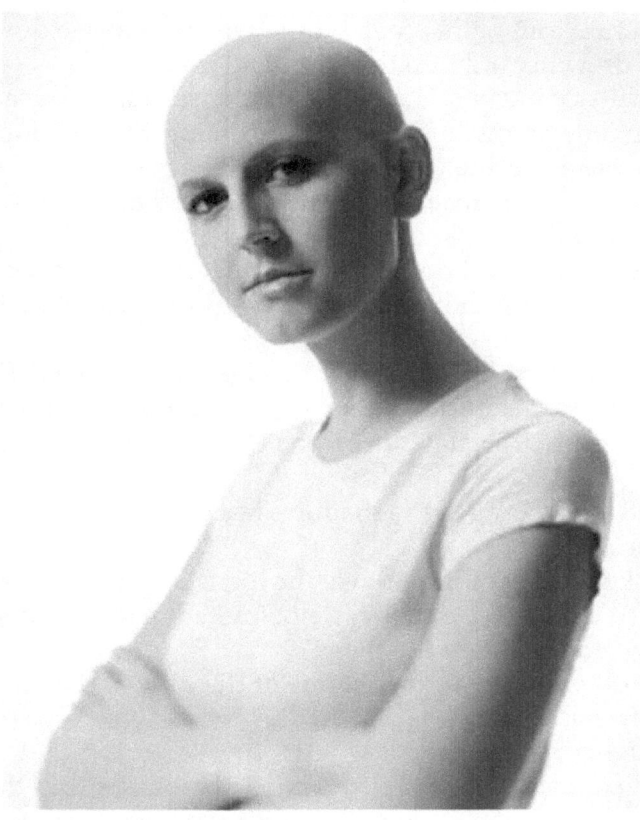

The drugs she was on made her weak, and the cold cut through her as it never could in the past. Deep it sank its claws when the wind blew, and she pulled her coat tight about her and shivered. Once she raced this hill to toboggan; laughing in the sunlight, she warred with snowball, and forged snowmen, cutting great Valkyrie figures in the snow. Now she huddled by the fence, staring into the dark woods and ice-girt river, silent and bitter, she listened to the night.

Her father had offered to the gods for her strength, called upon the Disir to guard her. Her mother had talked about staying positive, echoing the words of her coach, but the poison they called drugs wore upon her cheer as the sea wore upon the stone, until nothing was left but ruin. Her grandfather had battled this beast before, and lost great parts of himself to it, and spoke otherwise. When she turned away from the careful smiles, and forced cheer, she found her angry eyes locked with his cold wolf glare.

Grandpa Jim sneered, and flicked his eyes over her shoulders at the warm and laughing group to let her know it was they he sneered at. He carefully put on his coat, worked his way to the door with his cane, and drew her out into the night and silence.

He didn't look at her. They stood in silence, staring out at the trees. The evergreens by the house were welcoming as ever, but the silver maples by the fence line were long-clawed hags in winter, swaying in the wind, cold hands reaching for the light and life they were barred from, cold and hungry, and endlessly patient.

Slowly he stumped out to the tree line, and from his coat pulled a piece of meat from the feast, and split it in two. Half he handed to Jay, and half he kept.

"Svartly alfs, trolls, dark wights, night haunts, hail! Dark ones, hungry ones, spirits of the ice, know me. Hunter, I share meat from my table, a gift for the night, from one who knows you, and is known to you."

He cast his offering to the shadows beside the fence, into the dark. Jay did the same.

She asked her grandfather why he did this, since the spirits of the dark and cold were warded away, not invited in to hearth and home, and never had she offered to them.

"Why do you offer to the wights of the dark and cold, grandpa? Aren't they evil?"

He laughed, weakly.

"They are cold, hungry, bitter; cruel sometimes, but the night is not so dark, nor winter so cold, that it forgets love. There is hate here, bitterness, fear, hunger, rage, and honesty.

"I'm dying kiddo, and you might be too."

She shuddered, and the tears burned hot down her cheeks as he spoke the words she screamed into her pillow, but had been told and told again she must not even think.

"Sometimes you have nothing left, no strength, no hope, no joy, no love. Sometimes you are ready to give up, when all the light is gone."

He turned to her, and the shadows made his face a white skull with shadowed pits for eyes, the cold light of the moon and shadow painting him in colours of old bone and night.

"That is when the dark rises, that is when the night calls you. I am a killer, girl, I am a hard old man who has done terrible things and smiled when I did them. I know hate, and rage, and fear. The dark is in you girl, like it's in me. When the light is gone, when the hugs and love is not enough, when you have nothing left but the howl of your rage, and the hate rises to eat the fear: look to the dark."

"Winter is hard, girl. I am hard. Survivors have to be. Winter is a good teacher. There is no right or wrong, no good or evil, there is just survival and death. Winter and the dark can be cruel and cold, but nowhere is love as treasured as the dark, nowhere is loyalty stronger than at the edge of life. Nowhere will you know yourself as you do standing in the shadows, staring at your death from a heartbeat away."

Staring back at Grandpa Jim, her face was hard and cold as any blade he had used. He looked into the ice cold eyes, the hard line of her mouth drawn in a pale slash. He saw a fury in her, a rage. This one would not quit, this one would go kicking and clawing to the end, not a victim, but a fighter. His blood ran true. Those who had never faced the end helpless didn't know despair as he did, and she did. Only those who had lost it all could know the night, could learn the dark, and grow strong with it.

"Back to the light, girl, the night will be here when you need it. Winter is patient."

In the weeks that followed, her treatments grew harder. She went into hospital, and her strength faded. Bruising covered her, and her hair grew patchy, until she joked she was ready for the Zombie walk, and rather than laugh, her sister turned away to hide her tears.

Night came, and she looked upon the food before her, and looked out the window at the looming trees, great hag forms swaying, cold arms reaching for the light. Forever locked and barred from the light and hearth, forever waiting. She went to the locker, and stumbled into her clothes. When the nurses objected, she lied and told them

47

she was going for a cigarette, the only reason they would accept to let someone out into the snow and howling wind.

The cancer and the drugs had cost her much, and she no longer knew what was real, and what was hallucination. It didn't matter. Her father told her stories of ordeals, Odin's nine days and nights on the tree, the path of suffering as a key, the doors it unlocks in the mind, in the universe. Life shatters all your eggs, you may as well make an omelette. She laughed, and took the horrible eggs from the hospital tray. They would not feed her, but they would feed something. The night was hungry, winter was always hungry.

Away from the light she stumbled, into the dark. The cold cut through her, and she shivered. A teenaged pointe dancer's grace reduced to drunken stumbles, and a hockey player's strength to an old woman's weakness. She was an old woman, fragile and weak, wise in suffering, staring at an end that loomed closer with every breath, and fearing it less with every breath.

"Hail the wights of the dark, hail the svartly alfs, hail thee hungry ones. Accept my offerings."

She cast the eggs away, and a coyote slipped from the shadows, and eyed her. After a time the coyote was joined by three others, and all four devoured the offering. She looked up at the moon as the wind blew and the bare tree swayed, looking for a moment like a great hard limbed hag, with long claws striking down from the moonlight at her. She squeaked, and fell backwards to the snow. Looking into the eye like hollows of the tree, she heard a voice.

"Feeding us, calling us. Unwise. Weak are food. Only the fiercest survive long in the dark, only the hardest can outlast the cold."

Was it the fall? The drugs? The lack of sleep? Awake or dreaming, hallucinating or not, she saw the hard clawed tree-troll, the night hag looming black against the bone-white moon.

"Bring it!" snarled Jay, her teeth flashing white, spit flying from her bared teeth. Hands clenched in bone-hard fists, she lurched not away, but towards the looming shape, the fury rising in her, so long helpless, so long suffering, now at last, an enemy to face. In the killing cold, only the strongest fire burns. Jay burned.

The wind howled in answer, and the white snow lashed at the great hag, as if in answer to Jay's rising rage. The tree limbs straightened, swaying away again. The wind fell, and her strength spent, so did Jay. On hands and knees in the snow, shivering with cold and rage, she panted as she glared at the looming tree. Again the voice whispered from the dark trees.

"The winter is the dying time, when the light fails, hope fails, and the failing just stop fighting. But the hardest learn to do what they must, to fight harder, to endure what you must, and to never ever let go what is important. In the heart of the dark, in the killing cold, you can't do it alone. A gift for a gift little one, if you're hard enough."

The coyotes that had eaten her eggs were a mother and kits, and the little ones pressed tight against their mother when Jay looked and them. The mother stalked to the lee of the tree, and looked back; the kits followed, yipping. Jay crawled after, too tired to rise.

Beneath the dark trees were pools of white snow, shining bright in the harsh moonlight. One pool was black stained: a cat gutted and half chewed, the red snow of a fresh kill, made night dark in the winter light.

The hag's voice whispered again. Filling her mind, as the sight of the blood filled her eyes.

"Poison is in you, blight is in you. Death and blight to save you, for it is bright and growing life that destroys you. Death and blight alone can save you. You fight the poison that comes to save you, and the life grows and twists, and tears at you. Drink the dark, take the killing cold into you. Take the hunger, take the rage, take the spirit of red rage and white fangs. You are ours, and the winter is not so cold there is not room for love."

Knowing herself mad, and caring not, she drove clawed hands into the corpse and tore off still warm flesh. Hard it was to chew, and bitter to swallow. Black blood marked her lips, and cheeks, and soul. Red lips and white fangs flashed as she glared defiantly at the dark.

She turned and nodded to the coyote, who nodded in return before vanishing to the deeper shadows with her kits.

Back to her room she struggled, and fell deep into an exhausted sleep. Fever burned deep in her, as if a fire was lit in her flesh. The doctors were alarmed, but the fixed snarl and fevered fury gave her parents hope, for she was fighting again.

Week on week she fought; pumped with poison to save her life, filled with the blessing of the dark, the hungry killing cold, the bitter blood taste of brutal necessity. When she left the hospital at last, there was colour in her cheeks, and laughter again in her voice, most times.

When to her home she returned, a great feast they had to welcome her. The warmth and love was life affirming, and joyous. There were shadows in her eyes, and shadows in her moods, as one who has brushed the dark is never fully free of it, nor wants to be. When the light and laughter grew too much, she took from her plate a portion of meat, and slipped out into the night.

To the fence line she stalked, her steps stronger than last time. To the shadows between the dark and looming trees she threw her offering.

"Spirits of the dark, wights of the cold and night, svartly alfs, accept my offering. Blight and hunger, need and necessity, cruelty and suffering; for the gift of red snow I thank you. For the gift of fever, for the gift of hate, for the blight within, for the knowledge of endings, I thank you."

Bright eyes flashed from the shadows, watching and waiting for her to depart, before the feast begins. Winter is hunger, and patience.

Jay turned away, back towards the light and laughter of home. Granddad was right. The night would wait. Every light ended in darkness, every life in death. Those who had brushed the dark carried it with them always. Those who brushed the dark knew it had been with them always. Those who learned the darkness they held within them smiled less, and saw more.

From our homes we bar the baleful wights, but not from our lives entire. We light our homes, we light our world, but every light casts shadows, every day falls to night, every laugh ends in silence. The dark is with us, the baleful wights, the dark moods, the dark deeds, are in us. Wisest are they who know this, who learn the ways of the dark, and the dark in themselves. When light alone fails us, the darkness waits, hungry and patient, to teach those with the will to learn.

For all of those who have faced cancer,
or such faceless foes of body or mind.

A Little Lukey is Enough

Change is painful, fearful. Among the gods is one who is as often reviled as revered. Loki. Trickster, chaos bringer, and agent of change. History is kind to Hercules; everyone remembers his labours, everyone remembers the wonders he did, but only serious students of the lore remember each act of heroism was to atone for a wrong, sometimes a horrible one. Hercules was an agent of change, coming into a situation in stasis and shattering it, that something new could come to be. History is not as kind to Loki, who is more often equated with Lucifer than with Hermes, or Hercules; tricksters and bringers of change. This is a less than honest appreciation of his role in our lore. Loki was often journeying in the worlds with Odin and Thor. When they walked among men, the deeds they saw drew a response from the gods, for good or ill as the actions warranted. Frequently Loki was the one who was tasked with making the change. Change can be terrifying in the same degree it can frequently be necessary. Many times given any choice at all, we would avoid the cost of change, but Loki is a thief as well as trickster, and is not the greatest trick stealing our chance to avoid what we need?

Dave was "having trouble" adjusting back to civilian life since his return from Afghanistan. His wife told him this (just before she left), his physiotherapist told him this. The army told him he was no longer their problem as his prosthetic left arm was their last gift to him, just as they were taking from him the only community that he could talk to. The VA psychiatrists were "helping him" and a group of vets with "problems" to readjust.

It didn't help that the Army had let the preachers in. Absolutely the last thing a good heathen needed when trying to get a handle on his anger was having shrinks and missionaries double-teaming him while reminding him he couldn't ever be the warrior the gods called him to be. If it wasn't for that smart-ass Luke, or Lukey as he asked people to call him, he probably would have already exploded.

Being a good Thor's man, he had no time for double-talk, less for political correctness, such as seemed to be required for being deemed "well-adjusted" by the VA. One of the problems with convincing everyone that you were sane, was that none of people making the judgment about your sanity had any idea of what sights awaited him when he shut his eyes, what memories shaped his world, and what he had discovered he was capable of. Only the vets could understand his anger issues, and of those, only Lukey seemed to understand why he feared fire.

At the meeting, the head shrinker sat inset in the circle, to make it clear he was in charge, even while he pretended that everyone was equal. Everyone was forced to bow his head and listen to the preacher drone on his usual grovelling nonsense that already had Dave turning red and clamping his jaw with rage. He had enough trouble pretending he was still the man he used to be without some Bible thumper trying to call him a helpless lamb, and his dead helpless victims and not fallen warriors. He swore, if it wasn't for Lukey, this part would be enough to set him off.

There was one girl in the group, a Logistics Sgt who had made the papers back home. She and her partner had been caught in a Talib ambush. Seeking to hit the soft targets, they jumped a cargo truck driven by two women, and ended up getting a surprise. After a twenty minute firefight, the surviving Talib had pulled out their casualties leaving Sgt Karin Debruin with a wounded partner and six rounds in her last clip. She hadn't said a word in group since she got there, and everyone assumed her issues were PTSD from the firefight, but Dave wasn't so sure.

The starting prayer had ended, and Dave was ready to burst already. His Thor's hammer hung defiantly from his dog tags, in plain view of the disapproving preacher and counsellor. Lukey had the look of piety that (from him) meant he was bored enough to start something amusing, just to watch the explosion. "Buddy," as the counsellor liked to be called, was ready to start the "sharing", or randomly picking people to tell about their problems of the day, so that he could demonstrate how wrong their feelings were, and how normal people should think. Lukey had the look, he was not willing to wait for Buddy to pick someone, he had decided to have some fun, and Hel take the bystanders!

"Buddy," Lukey said, clasping his hands before him like a televangelist, "I have been thinking of all those poor people that I killed, and I just feel so terrible about it all. The guilt, it just keeps me from opening up and talking to anyone, just like Karin here."

Dave knew this was BS right from the start. Lukey was a joker, always smiling, always laughing, but his was a sarcastic gallows humour, an irreverent and capricious humour. His trade in the service was sniper, and as a consummate professional, he felt about as much guilt about servicing targets in combat as he did sharking people at the pool table. The damage was done though; all eyes fastened on Karin who looked caught in the attention like a rabbit by a rattlesnake.

Buddy began his probing of her, the tender conciliatory tones of a parent trying to talk a child off a ledge, or an owner trying to rescue a slipper from a teething pit bull. He talked about how hard it must be for a woman to live with the guilt, about how betrayed she must feel that she had to defend herself. He even went so far as to ask if her sex life suffered because she felt less feminine since "the incident".

Karin finally snapped, and began to answer in tones that began loud, and ratcheted right up into thunderous.

"How's my sex life? Well I tell you, getting back home to find that my beloved husband had moved in another woman to our home and our bed, and knocked her up while I was writing him letters every week dreaming of the chance to get home and start a family, pretty much ended that!

"Do I feel guilty? NO! I did my job, looked after my own, and to Hel with the frigging Talibs; they picked the ground and died on it.

"Why should I feel guilty?" She was screaming now. "I stayed faithful, did my duty, held on to our plan of starting a family, only to come home to see her decorating our nursery for her baby!"

While the rest of the men had the grace to look ashamed before her naked pain, Lukey was grinning his fox grin. Quietly leaning over, he whispered something to the preacher, who rose up and made the final mistake of the meeting.

"Dear child," the preacher intoned gravely, "you must give yourself to Jesus, and pray for forgiveness!"

Dave jumped out of his chair, shocked that anyone could be so crass and stupid at the same time with a woman who was clearly the wronged party by anyone's definition. Lukey was laughing and clapping like a child at the circus watching the clowns fall down.

Face streaming with tears, but voice thick and clear like a bell, Karin tore open her blouse, popping the first two buttons. At the curve of her cleavage over her left breast was a tattoo of three interlocking triangles, a symbol Dave recognized and Lukey clearly expected from his chortling, but one that meant nothing to the assembled group.

"This is a valknut, you moron!" she rasped at the preacher. "Odin's sign."

"My gods want my loyalty and my courage, not my forgiveness. Why can't I find a man who is loyal and brave enough to wait?"

She turned to rush from the room, and when the counsellor tried to stop her, Dave body- checked him out of the way, and he and Lukey rushed after her.

She had strode out of the conference room, straight out of the building, and was striding away from the rear parking lot, seemingly towards the pub at the other end of the block. Dave and Lukey caught up to her and bracketed her on the sidewalk. Between Dave's fierce glower and Lukey's predatory grin, no one on the night streets was foolish enough to comment on the distraught blonde with half-bared frontal armaments.

They found a booth in the bar and Dave ordered a pitcher. After cooling off a bit, Karin realized her state of undress and tucked her blouse in to make the cleavage more of a suggestion and less of an outright statement: the best that could be done without buttons. Dave shared his own marriage failure, while Lukey admitted to having had a wife in Afghanistan and one here too. Both Dave and Karin just shook their head, but Lukey seemed beyond the entire concept of shame.

Lukey strode over to the bar, and slipped the barman a twenty and some whispered instructions. He slid back to the booth and put an arm around Dave and Karin. He began with an apology for singling Karin out earlier, which should have been an alarm for both Dave and Karin, for Lukey feels no shame at all, unless it is required for dramatic effect. He went on to say that it was only fair he even the scales between her and Dave. Since we got to hear your dark secret and see your goodies, it's only fair that you get the same chance. Just as Dave opened his mouth to object, his gaze caught the waitress, and he froze, like a rabbit before a coiled rattler. As the waitress brought over the flaming Sambucca shooters Lukey had ordered, Dave was visibly shuddering.

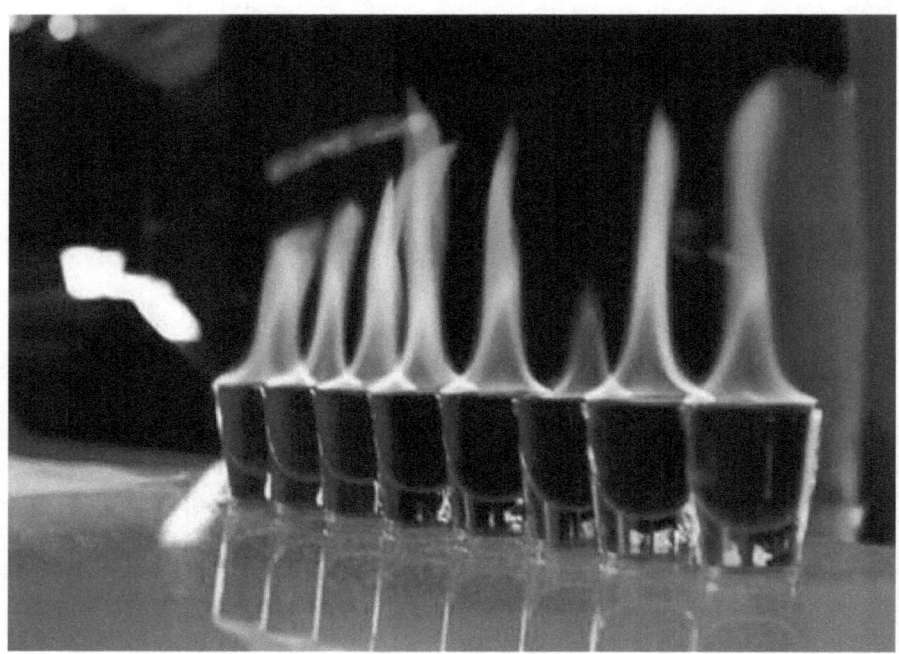

"Old Stumpy here got that hand in a little road misshap with an IED. Not all that unusual when you do as much convoy duty as Wax-Boy did. What makes our little wax hero over here different is when his vehicle got hit, it burned, baby." Lukey wove patterns with the flaming shot-glasses, painting signs and sigils with fire in the dark bar air.

"Now Stumpy here got himself out OK, but his driver was pinned inside, burning." Lukey gave Karin her drink, shot one, then mimed throwing one at Dave to make him flinch. When he threw up his stump to save his face, Lukey tore open Dave's shirt, revealing the white/pink layers of scar tissue, like melting wax that covered his chest.

"Our Dave here just wouldn't stop trying to pull out his buddies, even when he was on fire. I think that's just too stupid for words, right?"

Lukey looked over in sardonic amusement. As he thought, Karin's eyes were on Dave's. As he tried to hide the terrible scarring that had driven away his wife, the scars of his loyalty were no turn-off for a woman to whom loyalty was the first virtue. Lukey looked over at the soon-to-be couple as she ran her hands along his chest, stopping him from hiding his shame. As they gazed deeply into each other's eyes, he rolled his own.

Tossing back the two remaining flaming shooters he looked at the waitress.

"You know, they won't even invite me to the wedding. Shocking actually. Keep them pouring as long as they last, darlin'," Lukey drawled as he slapped some bills on the waitress' tray, and gave a quick slap on her rear. Her smile was halfway between amused and scandalized.

As Lukey started towards the door, a huge red bearded bouncer and the grizzled white bearded owner descended on him like two fullbacks, each taking an arm and escorting him to the door. The grey beard rasped, as gently as stone can get, "You've done enough, Lukey, time to leave them alone."

Lukey snickered and asked with the full false piety of before.

"You don't trust me? I am hurt."

The redbeard grunted with some humour.

"Not today. But a little Lukey is more than enough."

Mare

Change is something we do because we must. Sometimes we make changes that only we feel are necessary; we give up things, because we think we must, that were never asked for. We all have roles to play in this life; times call for us to put on a mask to succeed in a role or in a challenge that we have undertaken. The roles we play are real: student, soldier, lover, worker, teacher, leader, spouse, parent. There is a difference between the roles we play and the people we are. There is more to us than any one role, or even the sum of the roles we play.

Freyr, whose golden manhood we symbolically dance around as the Maypole each spring represents the male half of the fertile power of humanity. Lord of horses, lord of the herd, Freyr is the ever renewing, and his touch reminds us of our connection to the earth, to our primal selves, our bodies, our lives, and our joys. We give up so much that we think is required that we cannot afford to lose. It is his to remind us of who we are, and help us to become whole again.

Her name was Mary, but from the time she was two her father called her Mare. She loved it, as she loved three things in this world: her My Little Pony collection, her dancing, and working with her father in his workshop. He was big and strong, as her mother was slender and slight, and from him she learned to love working with wood, and learned the tools of his cabinetry as she learned her own toys.

She grew tall and coltish, her growth spurts making her frequently awkward as her body strove to do familiar dance moves with a body suddenly longer than it remembered, and she had to work harder to retain her skills than the other girls. Soon she was tallest by far, and that made her self-conscious. Being big and awkward made her hate her body before she had even grown into it. When her father died, the cancer from his eternal cigarettes carrying the day, she had to give up dance, but by then she had grown to hate the nickname "Mare" as it was used now as a cruel joke about the big horse of a girl she seemed.

High school saw her turn inward, without the dance community, again sitting so much taller than the other girls, and with her father's blunt speech made her not fit in much, save as a jock, where your performance mattered. She hit the gym and grew strong, strong as her father was. She felt comfortable in her body, but missed the joy of dance, and always dressed to conceal her body from others.

She had no luck getting the traditional girl jobs, as she loomed above her managers at the fast food places, and the fact she had to shop at men's stores for clothes that fit left her less than knowledgeable about the clothes in the trendy stores that were also hiring. In the end, she put on her work gloves, her steel toes, and her father's hard hat, and went to look for work in construction. A girl on the site was considered comical. Flag girls were OK, but a high school girl looking to work the trades was a joke!

They set her to the back-breaking tasks, hauling 4x4's for the framers, loading shingles on the conveyer for the roofers, humping the cement bags up the stairs for the concrete crews, and she didn't bat an eyelash. The first time an electrician tried to cop a feel as she was carrying a load resulted in three stiches and "Mare" suddenly shifting from the category of "girl on the jobsite" to tough construction worker. She was going to school studying drafting and learning about building codes, but her day job and focus was working construction. If she had no social life, and the dating scene seemed to have no one looking for six and a half foot women who could dead lift a Smart Car, well, that was just life.

The building inspections were finished by the city, but this contract was being run by a general contractor who wanted to look at the framing and electrical before the dry wall went up, as he had issues with some of the buildings elsewhere in the city. They had seen his business card posted at the steel grate elevator cage: F. Rey, Vanir

Industries. Mare had never seen him, but she had heard the stories. He was a great guy, a man's man, knew all kinds of stories, but he could spot substandard materials through two floors of concrete and could tell if a support was out of true better than a laser level.

He arrived in a hail of dust, his BMW screaming onto the site seemingly from highway speeds to a dead stop before the dust cleared to find him neatly in the reserved spot. He was blond, bearded, about six feet of long lean muscle and flashing grin. He wore a dress shirt of white silk that should have looked girlish but on him carried with it more overtones of pirate. He casually threw on a Hi Vis Engineers vest over his broad shoulders, and reached back in the convertible to come out with two stacks of doughnuts.

He came out of the boiler room, slapping the plumbing contractor on the back while the sprinker installation chief was swearing, holding a set of schematics covered with red circles and notes, showing the various differences between the "as built" drawings that were up to code, and the crap he could see actually installed. He never missed a chance to point out work that was well done, always jotting down the name of the contractors who met the mark, but he did the same with those he found wanting.

At the tenth floor he arrived to the cheers of the electricians; they knew him, and knew their work was up to his standards. He dropped his doughnuts and exchanged jests with the boys, then stopped dead.

There was a vision in front of him, a vision it seemed he alone could see. There was a woman—it was hard to tell with her bent in half in front of him, but she must top him by at least half a foot. Her curves were gentle womanhood, only written large. He saw the way she gripped the door frame, and held it slightly off the ground to bring it into perfect alignment with the slightly canted frame put in around the tenth floor fire box. She held the door frame with the ease of a strong man, double tapped the nail gun with the precision of a target shooter, yet the way she rose from her bend was like a dance move, or the stretch of a swan. Lost in his appreciation of her form, he couldn't help but note her joins were flawless, her nails flush and cleanly centered, without a single bruise on the wood or a raised edge.

"Who is that gorgeous creature?" said the inspector with the deep rumble of a voice no longer joking.

The job super looked confused, he didn't see any chicks here. Then he laughed, "Oh, that's just Mare. She's just one of the guys. Hell of a framer, pretty dab hand at cabinetry when I can't get my regular guy, but she's not like a real girl. She's, you know, Mare."

The king of all stallions looked upon her with approval and agreed. "She is indeed."

He was joking with some of the contractors when she punched out and headed across the site to the skytrain and home when she heard the cute inspector call out.

"Mare, hold a second!"

She didn't think he had any reason to talk to her, I mean not everything on the site was perfect, but her work—not just the internal wood work, but all the trades of the building envelope—were as good as she had ever seen. She turned, flicking her long dark ponytail over one shoulder and eyed him carefully.

She was perfect. Tall and strong, she moved with grace and economy. Taking half the steps of most of the people, she seemed to glide across the site. When she turned, the casual flick of her ponytail made his inner stallion snort and rear, and when she turned, the light caught her profile. Her posture had the sort of slump that some tall people adopted to fit in with lesser beings, but when she wasn't paying attention, she stood tall and spear straight. When she turned just now, her body swayed like willow caressed by the wind, and the light behind her silhouetted a high breasted form, long limbs deeply tanned and toned with the promise of youth and power, grace and stamina. She was a Mare, she was feminine grace and power in a world filled with men too lacking in power to rise to the challenge she implied.

He began by praising her work, and making it clear that his reports had already been filed, that his work was done here hours ago. He had waited to talk to her. She was confused, and flattered. Nobody looked at her that way. I mean they flirted with the lunch truck lady and she was 50, and the flag girls all got it, but no one looked at her that way, except the creeps she put the fear of herself into. He asked her out to dinner, which had her look down at her dirty work clothes and over at his tailored suit, and yes you really can get Italian leather steel toes if cost is no object.

As she opened her mouth to object, he told her right off that he would drive her home to shower and change first, he had lots of emails and phone calls he could catch up on while she was doing that, but then he stopped and looked her in the eye and said:

"But when we go out, the phone gets shut off. When we go out, there is no one else in the world but the two of us."

It should have felt corny, but it made her blush in a way she hadn't done since grade school. She looked into his blue eyes and she remembered how she used to feel when she was dancing, she remembered being a little girl with her parents watching, and wearing a little flower crown as she danced with her ribbon around the May Pole when dancing made the whole world sing to her. She said yes.

When the time came for dinner, he ordered the steak and lobster, and she did the same, as they made small talk and tore into the little breads brought to balance the wine while you waited for food. He told her what a relief it was to have a woman who could eat on a date, and not pretend she lived on two pieces of lettuce and a single cheese curd. She looked self-conscious for a second, but he laughed and said that he was a man of hearty appetites, and nothing pleased him more than someone who was unafraid to embrace life, to live fully and utterly as who they were, to eat when they were hungry, dance when they were joyful and get their hands dirty to take a dream from their head and make it real with their own two hands. She looked down at her plate, a blush stealing over her, and she muttered that she gave up dancing years ago, it made her uncomfortable when others were watching her. He laughed, and brought over the wine bottle to top up her glass. When she raised her eyes to watch him pour she saw him watching.

"When you dance from now on, you will know I am watching."

She took a drink and felt herself caught up in a storm of emotion, unable and unwilling to control it, but more than ready to see where it would carry her.

They ate, and they talked. Then they caught a cab to a club where his name was enough to get them past the lineup and into the packed club where they danced. She lost herself in the dance, as she never had for years. Her body moved with the grace and skill of long years of training, the awkwardness of teen growth long lost in the discipline of years of hard work and balance in dangerous places. She let go, and watched him do the same. His moves were challenging, like a king stag in the glen, his every move caused the women on the dance floor to notice him, and the men to back off muttering rather than challenge him. Every eye was on them, but she cared not, for she felt only his eyes on her, and his eyes for her alone.

She grabbed his hand and took them from the dance floor. His hotel was closer, and soon in their passion they had torn their clothing from each other. She stood before him naked, and reached in her head for the awkwardness her size and strength had brought in her youth. The childlike joy when her father called her Mare had long been replaced by the mockery and scorn of her schoolmates and dance-mates using Mare to mock her clumsiness and size. She learned a third meaning now. Frey looked upon her with shining eyes, threw back his head and called in a voice low and challenging "Mare." She reached for him and whispered in his ear before she bit it, "Stallion".

There was definitely something up at the jobsite. Everywhere she walked, conversations would stop, two men spilled their own coffee, and one of the scaffolding guys walked right into an upright watching her walk past. She was dressed exactly the same, but there was something different, something powerful in her walk, a sway that was never there before.

A horn honked from the entrance way, and Frey's BMW screamed into the lot. Mare swayed over to meet it. F. Rey the Inspector hopped out, donned his engineering vest, and picked up a second hard hat. This one was gleaming stainless, with a golden running horse emblazoned on each side above the sound-cancelling headphones, and MARE stamped upon the brim.

"Here you go, my dear." He pointed to a compartment in the back. "You plug your iPod in there and you can have music while you work all day. It automatically picks up any human speech, so you hear people better than without them on. Now you can dance while you work." His last words carried the uncomplicated smile of a man who enjoys the woman he is looking at.

Mare plugged in her iPhone, tossed her old hat in his back seat, and stepped forward. He grabbed her head and pulled her down for a long kiss. She reached around, grabbed two firm handfuls of his ass, and pulled him right off the ground, and into the kiss. Wolf whistles sounded from all around until she let him down again.

As he drove away, she moved the earmuffs on, and moving to the music that only she could hear, took up her lunch box and tool belt and headed for the elevator. The sway of her ponytail and the sway of her hips caught every eye.

"Frack me," the Superintendent muttered to the flag girl. "Mare is girl!"

The flag girl slapped him in the back of the head with her stop sign and stalked off in disgust, muttering, "Men. . . ."

Odinsball Saga: The Tale of Kenneth's Left Hairy Nut

Change is not always about what is gained or lost, but what we fear we have lost. Love is an important connection to life. Love is an important connection between people. The act of love-making is profoundly life affirming, and the source of life itself. It is not, however, an act of power in and of itself. Lovemaking is a symbolic act when it joins two people together who love each other. There is the physical aspect that is both immensely pleasurable, there is an emotional aspect where the reciprocal gift of pleasure serves to deepen the ties between lovers, there is the spiritual act of mingling two souls on several levels.

Things can happen in life that damage our ability to express this love in physical form. There is a fear in both men and women that the inability to function in the life generating capacity of our gender makes us less of a man, or less of a woman. To be barren, sterile, or impotent is not only a threat to our sense of self, but to our perception that we can contribute to the relationships of the people we love.

Fear is real. The fear of what "might be wrong" has become more of a problem in relationships than the facts of what is actually wrong (if anything) ever could be. In any relationship involving two human beings involved in romance, the potential for both tragedy and comedy is implicit. Ours are not safe gods to worship, for a being with the ability to see our wants, our needs, and the unfolding potential of our choices that also possesses a sense of humour is a terrifying concept.

For those who think they know the incident in question: yes, I changed the details of people and places involved. No careers were harmed in the making of this story.

There is a law, an ancient and hoary law called the "Law of unintended consequences" which the Norse were wont to explain in ancient times by saying wyrd is weird (in response to odd news, usually followed by belching explosively and drinking again). This law interacts strangely with reality and creates tales that stretch and grow beyond the facts themselves, until reality just gives up and sulks in the corner, while the tale and the life it took on caper madly across the world stage.

Sgt Kenneth Stones (aka Stoney) was a Badger commander with the 1st Combat Engineering Regiment, 11 Field Squadron (1CER, 11 Field) attached to the Lord Strathcona Horse (LSCH or Strats) Armoured Regiment deployed with the ISAF. The job of the 1CER ranged from the endless battle to clear the 15 million mines emplaced throughout Afghanistan, as well as the constant stream of IED that were replacing them, all the way through civil engineering projects with Provincial Reconstruction Teams attempting to rebuild the water and food distribution networks largely destroyed and ignored through generations of war.

There was a right way and a wrong way to do mine clearing: the right way was steady and patient, the wrong way was quick and dirty. The order of the day was Operation Hoover; a joint thrust by Canadian armour (the Strathcona Horse) and a herd of handless cows, also known as the Afghan Army. Any operation involving the ANA is plagued with the twin problems of officers who need to demonstrate their command in utterly counterproductive ways, usually involving adding delays, or random screaming, and the seemingly random actions of its troops who manage to divide at every intersection, and randomly surge and stop on any road move, usually forcing NATO troops into danger just to keep them from ending up soft kills.

The road between Kandahar base and Zhari was frequently mined, and the buildup for the push into Zhari was well known, as anything told to the ANA was generally better known to the line fighters of the Taliban than the NCOs of the ANA itself. To balance the utter lack of strategic and tactical surprise, the heavy use of drone reconnaissance, and manned light reconnaissance from the Dragoon elements served to limit the amount of time the insurgents had to prepare buried surprises, and the Leopard 2 tanks of the Strats served to deter anyone who thought about direct fire resistance. This left dealing with those surprises that did get emplaced to the Engineers.

After a day of random stops for screaming, overheated trucks of the attached ANA, and two routine detections of suspected mines, the drone/squeal of track and endless dust of the road to Zhari had made hard inroads into everyone's awareness. For that reason, the Strathcona commander was slow in seeing the four Afghan trucks decide to shift out of the dust of the preceding Leopard tanks, and move to the shoulder of the road, and out of the dust. This also put them outside the cleared zone, and into a mine field.

The first shock of fire brought everyone to alert. The radio exploded with calls as tanks deployed, turrets swiveling over their assigned sector like hounds tasting the air for prey. The Afghan trucks in the main column acted seemingly at random. Some ANA collided with the back of the stopped tanks, some dodging and continuing down the road, and some surging to the sides of the road and into the areas already proven to be mined.

Anticipating the order, Stoney turned his Badger, and began to sweep/clear towards the stricken ANA trucks, the three that were not yet on fire. Clearing up to the stricken vehicles, his Badger came under 14.5mm fire as concealed heavy weapons began to seek the soft ANA targets. Moving his armour between the helpless ANA and the machinegun emplacement, his hull rang like Thor was demanding to be let in. The booming response of the big Leopard's 120mm and stutter of the co-ax 7.62 let him know that the machine gun fire was not going to be a problem for long. Just as he thought he was safe, a RPG hit the track of his Badger. The explosion ruptured something in his track, and he felt a terrible pain in his nuts.

In the hospital he received the news: he had lost a testicle when a fastener had spalled off the inside of his track. He had lost a nut, to a nut. "Holy Odin, does my other nut work?" He and his wife Deanne were trying to have a baby between deployments, and he didn't even want to think of life nutless. The thought was disturbing on a whole lot of levels. The doctor, a female Captain, simply smiled and said that as far as she could tell, the right one still looked fine.

Barber knew Stoney had got hit. RUMINT (rumour intelligence) had it that he had had his nuts shot right off. Stoney was one of the Heathens that he got together with to tell stories, and offer bad IMPs (Individual Meal Packs) to the local wights and gods in between missions. The thought that Stoney had lost his stones worried him. He knew Stoney was trying to have a kid, and this would really screw him up. He made the trip over to the Strats area in Zhari when they laagered, and got the straight story that he had lost only his left nut.

One of Stoney's favourite curses was "Odin's left hairy nut," and now he had lost his. Graeme had a sense of humour which hadn't quite got him shot, and had made him a lot of friends. He decided to make a little something for his buddy. During the firefight (about six seconds of fun) some Taliban were rendered into component parts, one truckload of ANA were roasted, and a couple of goats were killed. This clearly called for goat. Taking his knife he cut out a big patch of goat hide, and began scraping it off. When his buddies asked what he was doing, he let them know that "Stoney lost his left nut, so I am going to sew him a big hairy one."

Stoney was a popular figure, so the idea had traction. Soon Dieter, Stoney's driver came over with a blue garnet, the size of a child's fist. Dieter loved to carve, and he had clearly been working on this piece. He had engraved the Odin's valknut on the stone. Granted, due to the nature of garnet it was a fairly jagged and uneven carving, but just gave it a little more punch.

"Barber, you jackass," Dieter opened with the usual pleasantries. "I hear you are going to sew Stoney a hairy left nut." Bouncing the light-catching garnet in his hands, he tossed it to Barber.

Barber turned the stone over, and took in the carving and the way it caught the light. This was something that Dieter had oathed he would do at sumbel some time ago: to make an offering for Odin from the stones of this place, because these stones had already received too much Canadian blood sacrificed already. While soldiers can have their serious moments, it was important to not take things too seriously, or at least be seen to, so both guys played like the gift was nothing special.

"Cool," said Barber.

Sewing two layers of goat skin around the blue garnet, Barber decided to keep the Odin motif by burning Ansuz runes into the goatskin nut-sack. The whole thing was about the size of a stress ball, and its fuzzy shape was oddly comforting to fidget with. Stoney would like it.

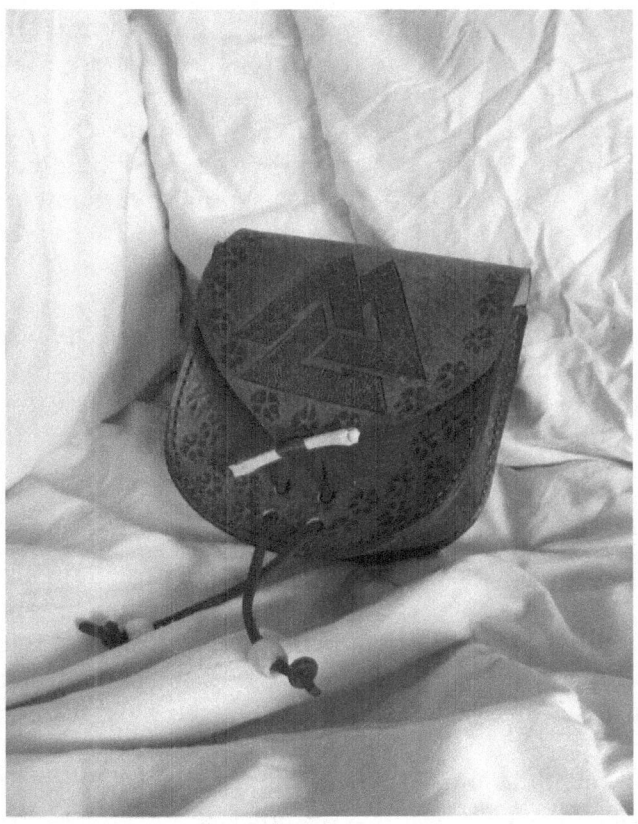

Sgt Stones was making the hardest Skype call of his life, to tell his wife Deanne about his injury. Looking into her smiling face, and cute blonde braids he felt a cold fear settle into his guts. His wife was the central joy of his life and their dream of a family was what kept him going. He saw the shock drain the colour from her face as he described getting hit, and that he had lost his left testicle.

"Baby," she said, "is everything OK, you know, down there?"

She saw the sick fear leaching all expression from his face, until it was his blank war mask staring back at her. Realizing what he was afraid of, and that she had made it worse, she scrambled to recover.

"It's OK, baby, I love you either way."

When he ended the call, she got worried and called the SSM's wife. In the way of most military, the senior NCO wives became the resource for the rest of the unit's families when things went sideways, either at home, or with their service people in the field.

Reaching the Squadron Sgt Major's wife, she got her news out in a rush:

"Connie, I think I fucked up. Kenneth got wounded in the groin and lost a testicle, and we are trying to start a family. When he told me, I didn't really think, and before I had a chance to really process it, I had already asked if he could, you know, function.

"Oh Connie, he went so cold, and hung up right after. I'm afraid that something is wrong, and that he is going to do something stupid if it all doesn't work down there, and it's GOING TO BE MY FAULT!"

She was screaming towards the end, and there was a long moment of silence before Connie responded.

"Fuck me gently," Connie replied; she knew exactly what Deanne was talking about. Manhood was really important to the guys, and the smartest of them did really stupid things when they thought they had failed, or were no longer "real men." Mostly it was with psychological problems, but injuries from IED had caused a few as well. Some of the guys had ended eating their guns over it, so the wives and girlfriends learned to walk carefully around some subjects.

"Deanne, you need to put a call in to the chaplain's office right now, and let them know. You know he's not going to talk to any of the head shop—" psychiatrists being not universally able to speak soldier, talking to them usually resulted in the soldier being told he was being irrational or foolish in his concerns, which really didn't help.

"I will call Bill, and see if he can get his buddies to talk him through this." It was best to keep things in house, and her husband Bill, the SSM, would be able to get Ken straightened out before things got bad.

Kenneth was in a really bad place in hospital when Barber arrived. Stoney could really shut down when he was thinking about something, and it looked like he was in full lockdown when Barber strolled in. That was OK; Barber knew the right way to deal with somebody afraid to talk was to poke them with a stick until they exploded, and then laugh about it afterwards.

"Yo! Stoney!" Barber opened. "You dropped something at Zhari, and Dieter picked it up for you. Catch!"

On a paracord necklace was a goatskin ball about the size of a baseball. It was surprisingly heavy when he caught it, and oddly textured. As Ken squeezed the odd hairy ball, Barber continued.

"Compliments of the Zipperheads of the Lord Strathcona, and the superior Recce troopers of the Dragoons, I give to you Stoney's Left Hairy Nut. You always swore by Odin's left hairy one, so we made you one of your own. Cheers, buddy"

Kenneth sat there honestly not knowing what to say for several seconds, then looking from the heavy nutsack in his hand to Barber's grinning face, something broke inside him, and he began to laugh. Soon tears were running down both their faces, and Kenneth hung the paracord necklace around his own neck. As Barber left he cautioned Kenneth:

"Be careful man, we all got together and blessed that fucker, that is one powerful nut. If you aren't careful you are going to knock up half the nursing staff, or sack Kabul or some shit." Placing his hands upon his chest, and adopting a pious pose, he continued: "Use its power wisely, young padawan."

Kenneth, laughing ,flipped him the bird, and shouted at the retreating trooper, "Get back to work you lazy bastard!"

Kenneth was feeling a lot better now, as he sat in the bed fingering the odd hairy package.

Connie had been thinking about the big problem of male ego. The big thing was, Kenneth needed to know if the equipment worked or not, and couldn't fail in front of Deanne. The obvious solution was not something she felt all that good about suggesting, but she had seen how really badly the situation had gone when a returning soldier had failed with his loved one, and not been prepared for it. She decided that this was a two bottle conversation. One to get them loose enough to talk about the fears both women held, and the second to make Connie's solution sound reasonable. She would get her kids to sleep over with one of the other wives, because she couldn't do Monday morning school prep with a hangover, and she could not get them drunk enough for this reason without being hung over. One trip to the base liquor store, and she was ready.

Half way into the second bottle, and all the way into the bag, Connie broached her plan.

"You know sweety, the problem is Kenneth loves you too much. You know that, right? He is going to be under so much pressure to be a man for you that even if the equipment still works, he might have, you know, issues."

Connie made flopping motions with her hand, and Deanne nodded gravely, with the seriousness of the deeply drunk.

"Men can be such babies about that," Deanne admitted.

Connie went on, driving directly at her point.

"If only we could let him test drive it with some bimbo, just to make sure it still worked, then he could come back without being all worked up. If there was a problem, he wouldn't be freaking out in front of you, you could, you know, prepare for it."

"He needs a hooker!" said Deanne, "Oops, is that bad? That is bad. It's not a bad idea though. . ."

Connie pretended surprise,

"Oh my god, you are totally righ! I'll totally call Bill right now and get it set up. He can totally get him a week's leave in Bali between the hospital and going back to the field."

Actually, she had done THAT the night before.

Bill had decided he needed to talk to some of the single guys to find out how to get Stones' tubes cleaned on leave. Being married, he had been trying to avoid doing that kind of research himself, and it really needed to be done by somebody who was ready to deal with possible issues. He figured to enlist Barber and Dieter; they were both known poon-hounds, although Dieter had been off the wagon since getting engaged.

Kenneth's orders for leave came through, just after the notation that he had been put in for an award for saving the ANA soldiers in the ambush. As he was getting loaded up into the plane, the OC for the squadron along with the SSM came with a group from HQ. In the airport, the OC called the group to attention, and read out Kenneth's formal mention in dispatch for bravery, noting he had been put in for an award of valour. The stewardesses were impressed by the ceremony, and Barber snuck his way over and began chatting them up. He made a big deal about Stoney's bravery, but let out the secret that his after losing his nut, he was afraid to face his wife, not knowing if everything still worked. He told the stewardesses that they were afraid he might do something terrible because he was afraid to face her not knowing. Then he shifted subjects and pulled out the collection the brigade had taken up.

"Say, we took up a collection for Stoney. Could you girls get him bumped to first class, and see he's taken care of. I mean, he means the world to us, and we would hate to lose him."

Pushing a wad of Canadian and US dollars, with a few British pounds mixed in (Stoney was popular with a lot of the troops) into the stewardesses' hands, he gave them a deeply innocent look. The stewardesses shared a smile, and assured him with their Indonesian accents that they would look after his brave friend "very well."

The regular CF Chaplain was aware that Sgt Stones was Asatru, but due to his attachment to the Strats, that little item got missed, and a regular, earnest Christian chaplain from the Strats was tasked to seek out the soldier on the airplane and make sure of his mental state, prior to his being released for a week of leave in Bali. He didn't see the soldier in his assigned seat, and decided there must have been a seating change. Being a terribly earnest chaplain, he decided to pray for a while to settle himself before seeking out this challenging counselling case. Usually he knew the soldier a little, or had at least a good background on him from the Regimental Orderly Room. This was all unknown for him, and therefore more challenging. He prayed for guidance.

Kenneth was enjoying first class. Two stewardesses kept bringing him scotches, saying they had been paid for by his friends in Afghanistan, and Ken was more than a little drunk. Each time they came, they would touch the little goatskin bag on his chest, and giggle. Ken began to wonder if Odin's left hairy nut was the thing for a married man to hang around his neck while on leave, but then he thought it might not matter to him at all, and drank harder.

As the flight wore on, the stewardesses came and closed the curtains around the soldier, and told him that it was customary for first class passengers to receive a massage in flight. He had never travelled first class, so he found this amazing. They asked him to remove his shirt and lie back. Both girls also removed their coats and began to massage him. There was a lot more giggling than he thought was part of a massage, but he noticed it felt VERY good. When he opened his mouth to object, one or the other would give him another sip of scotch, and soon he was feeling far too good for his own good.

Kenneth was aware that things were not going properly when his pants came off, and so did the stewardesses' tops. He attempted to explain that he was married, but when he opened his mouth and turned to explain, he found his face buried between two golden breasts, and when he raised his hands to push them away, the stewardess guided them giggling to places a married man's hands shouldn't be on someone other than his wife.

The second stewardess was curious to see if the wounded soldier's remaining nut matched the great hairy one hanging on his chest, and with a certain amount of giggling had assured herself that it was indeed there, and working, for the young soldier was standing proudly, and possibly painfully, to full and rigid attention. She was beginning to say hello to the soldiers' side-arm when Kenneth rather drunkenly announced from between the breasts of the first stewardess, "No, wait, I can't, I'm married!"

This would be where wyrd gets weird, for it would be at this moment that the errant chaplain had succeeded in finding where his missing soldier had been seated. As he approached the drawn curtains, he pulled them open with a ready smile in one hand, and his Bible clutched in the other. The sight that greeted him became the stuff of Regimental legend. Stg "Stoney" Stones lay wearing only the hairy rune-marked goat skin nut-sack and his dog tags, with only one stewardess's head to cover his nakedness, and a second stewardess's charms obscuring his face.

"Jesus Christ! What in God's name is going on?!?" the priest roared in bewildered rage.

"Odin's Left Hairy Nut!" Kenneth roared in drunken surprise and embarrassment.

"*Kotran!*" (Shit!) swore the two stewardesses, as they raced to quickly dress and leave.

Kenneth swore that he would never cheat on his wife, as he strove to stuff the offending part of his anatomy back in his uniform pants, but it was neither bending, nor co-operating in the whole dressing procedure. He swore again and again: "Its Odin's left hairy nut, they put too much juice in, it made the stewardesses crazy and made me cheat on Deanne!"

He waved the offending nutsack at the priest, who noticed the hammer hanging on the Sgt's dog-tags, and realized he was not a good Christian, but some form of heathen, and that the ball sack he was waiving was some sort of heathen sex-magic. Seeing his duty to God to save this soldier from Satan, he told him to give him the cursed object now and beg Jesus for forgiveness, or he would see him charged with Conduct Unbecoming, and have a long talk with his wife.

Kenneth accepted a scotch from the apologetic stewardesses, and raised it to the sky.

"Odin, get my ass out of this without charges or a divorce, and I swear I will offer to you every Wednesday for the next year!"

The stewardesses were worried the priest would get them fired, as Christians were such drama queens that way. They were good Hindu girls, and found the Christian priests to be hypocritical creepy pervs at the best of times, and having this one sitting there trying to exorcize the goat skin ball sack was seriously upsetting the passengers. The captain summoned them to the cockpit to find out what the problem was. When they explained, the captain laughed and asked if the head stewardess still had the roofies that she confiscated from the man in 17C. The girls' eyes lit up, and they saw the only possible way out of their problem.

Asking the priest to accept an upgrade to first class to be with his soldier, they brought him a complementary special coffee. Coincidentally, this got the chanting madman away from the rest of their passengers.

After his coffee, the chaplain, who had been having an overly stressful day, began to get really confused. For some reason he was really hot, and the stewardesses were helping him take off his clothes. They were taking off theirs too, so it must really be hot on this plane. They put the demonic necklace on him, and began to touch him places. He put his hands down there to stop them, and the girls giggling guided his hands until they were moving up and down; hey, this felt pretty good.

The stewardesses faithfully recorded pictures of the chaplain comforting his rod and staff, while dressed only in the necklace: Odin's Left Hairy Nut.

Before beginning the descent, the captain himself had come back to wake the sleeping chaplain and ensure his crew's safety from official fallout. With his sternest paternal face, he woke the sleeper. Beside him was the matronly chief stewardess.

"Sir, I'm afraid that you have been behaving strangely. If you will look at the pictures on the chief stewardess's phone, you will see that you removed all of your clothing, and with one hand on the furry testicle charm, began to touch yourself"

The chaplain was not entirely over the effects of his drugs, and was extremely easily led at this point. The firm fatherly tones of the captain, and the harsh disapproving looks of the chief stewardess made him curl up in shame, and seek for any excuse to preserve his dignity. The stewardess offered him an out.

"This necklace is very strong, filled with much sexual power by an ancient god. Good Hindu know the lusts of the gods are too strong for mortals to handle alone. I don't think your god gives such love magic to his priests. Maybe it would be safer for you to return it to the soldier that it was given to heal, and forget any of this ever happened. This was given to work a powerful cure on a soldier, and it is no fault of anyone if mortal people became caught up in the work of the gods."

The old stewardess knew that ass covering was a reflex among all men of power, and any excuse, regardless of how thin, would suffice if it meant the man in question is not responsible for whatever he was caught doing.

"Jesus Christ!" the chaplain said as he extended the necklace to the smiling stewardess. The captain smiled, knowing that the chaplain would not make any official waves over this, and all careers were saved.

With all due ceremony, the chief stewardess walked down the aisle of first class from the Stewards area. Behind her marched the rest of the stewardesses. In her hands was a pillow, and upon that pillow sat the paracord necklace, and Odin's Left Hairy Nut.

The jaded members of first class, having spent the whole flight gossiping about the goings on, began to applaud wildly. With great seriousness, the chief stewardess offered the Sgt his necklace. As he placed the necklace over his head, the remaining stewardesses showered him with flower petals recently stripped from their stash of guest gifts. As each stewardess passed they gave him a chaste kiss upon the cheek, leaving him blushing bright crimson, and the whole of first class cheering.

Nothing official came of it, but RUMINT travels faster than light, and distorts more than a little in transmission. By the time he returned, the saga of Sgt Stoney's Left Hairy Nut had grown. At every gathering of heathens, and most gatherings in the field, the troops would demand the Left Hairy One be brought out, with everyone touching it for luck.

The remainder of the rotation went smoothly, and the return to Edmonton was finally achieved. Connie admitted to a certain amount of smugness when Kenneth and Deanne emerged from the return stronger as a couple, and with a good handle on dealing with the issues that always attend returning from a deployment. When Deanne announced less than a month after the return that she was expecting a baby, the legend of the Left Hairy Nut passed into permanent regimental lore. The first request from a wife to borrow said necklace to "help things along" in their family planning followed shortly thereafter.

Bears and BS

I had been back for about two months. When you are Reserves and get deployed, it works a little differently than Regular Army. You come back from Over There (whichever version of bad thing is currently sucking up our blood and treasure), and they kick you free into your civilian life. There is a hunger to get back to normal, to get the white picket fences, the drive through coffee, the ability to get good Chinese delivered at 0200hrs on a Wednesday. Hearth and home, that's what you hold in your mind, get back to hearth and home. Then you get back.

The first month is mentally the hardest. Everyone is on eggshells around each other, trying so hard to Make It Work. The kids are the hardest, because they don't think at all, they say exactly what is in their minds and hearts and they get to you. Their world has changed, not a little bit; in their world a good portion of their life has happened while you were gone, and every little thing that is different slaps you in the face. My wife is trying hard, but I think she cries as much now that I am back, as when I was gone. She hates resenting me for all the things she had to face alone, and I hate resenting her for all the things she got to be a part of while I was gone. We love each other, but there is an anger building that I just can't deal with.

Nights get bad. Dreams start opening boxes in my head I closed for a reason. When you are deployed, you bottle things up. It's not like the movies; there are not single tragic things that we wake up thinking about. Honestly, the parts most people fixate on don't bother me; the stuff you could action got dealt with, we got closure. The parts that get bottled up are the stresses, the near misses, the stuff you laugh off because it "don't mean shit". You stick it in little boxes to deal with later. Two months is later. There are times when something happens, something small and stupid, and my reactions scare the crap out of me, and the fear I see in their eyes scares me more. Adrenaline, it is a heartbeat away; the rage, the instant ability to go to alpha state, to bring 100% of my skills and training to bear is one heartbeat away, and there is no external threat to use it on. Looking in the mirror, I wonder if I am looking at the threat.

I am heathen. Sure when you ask me about it, I will talk a lot about the virtues, the ethics, the codes of conduct and how they are part of what makes me the man I am, and how important those teachings are to me. Over There they kept me sane, because while my life to that point had no context for what we had to do, how we had to live, the lore, the gods, ancestors, and wights of the land gave me context and connection. They gave me anchors, purpose, allowed me to be me, and still be what I needed to be for everyone else. It wasn't about doing the job; we could all do the job, it was about being OK with it, about feeling good about muddling through a crappy situation in which nothing we could do would make things a lot better, but screwing up could make things a lot worse. Laughter is like gold, when you can feel happy at the little things, do little things for each other and have good times, no bullshit, really good days in a really bad place, it makes everyone around you feel better, cope better, and perform better. I don't go for a lot of the "Woo-woo" magic stuff, it's just not me. Nothing against those types, but it's not something I get. Being Heathen was part of what kept me together over there, and I had a feeling that the urge building in me to GET AWAY was coming from that heathen part.

We had a fight. Things were said. I got our daughter ready for school, and she burst into tears because I missed something that was part of the routine, something special they did to remind each other that they loved each other. I didn't know anything about it, because they began it, mother and daughter, while I was training for deployment, and kept it religiously while I was deployed. I was the reason, yet I was left out. I handled it badly. Things were said. That I can't take back. I grabbed my sidearm from the nightstand, and took the trigger lock off it. I didn't really think about why. I had to get away, from me, from them.

I told my wife I was headed up the mountain. She asked when I would be back, but I didn't answer.

I took the truck up Old Yale Road, up to the old forestry access road. There is a gate, but it got soft on the side of the road and the posts leaned outward, so it didn't quite reach the lock anymore, so you could just swing it open these days. No one went up here outside of hunting season. The bears and moose pretty much had it to themselves. The trails were not maintained, and the forest was dark and pretty treacherous to walk. Search and Rescue hated the mountain; its sight lines sucked, and there were few features to navigate on easily. I called it a Yuppie Free Zone. No yoga pants had ever touched this mountain, and that was pretty much OK by me. I wanted to get away.

I got to a pull off on the road, originally a run-away lane for logging trucks, and stopped the truck. I got out. I took the side arm out of the glove box, and walked over to a copse of trees. A big fir had died here long ago; you could park a car in the stump, and three of its children branched off its corpse, covering it with a net of hard roots that looked like a moss-covered throne or high seat. I sat and thought. The gun was in my hand, and my thumb stroked the safety almost without thought. I was angry, so very angry. At her, at myself, at life. My lips were white and drawn tight against my teeth, as even my face was hard and drawn. I just couldn't take it anymore. I had been back two months, I guess, that's all it takes to get rusty. I guess it's good I never screwed up that bad over there, because I clearly heard the click of a safety, and it was not mine.

"What in the nine worlds do you think you are going to do with that pistol on my mountain, son?"

I turned carefully to look at the muzzle brake of a rifle that looked like it was designed to cull the tank population when they went into season. Tracking slowly down the cannon to the hands that held it: they were scarred, hard, long fingered, and old. The rifle must have weighed a good thirty or forty pounds, but he held it casually just off line of the sniper's triangle, with the casual ease that suggested its swift pivoting over my breast bone should my answers fail to please him. He was dressed in an old battered winter camo coat, a blue/grey pattern that spoke of ice and rock and empty high places. His hair was grey, wild, and half covered his face, but the smile on it was wry and knowing. The eye that was on me was one that had seen it all, and wasn't impressed by much of it. He seemed to find something deeply amusing in sitting here, at gunpoint with an angry young man on the mountain.

I put my pistol slowly down on the roots, and he swung his rifle down to order arms, and leaned casually on it like a walking staff. He could, it was certainly tall enough to pass as a staff or spear. I don't know why, because I don't do this, but I found myself spilling pretty much everything. By the end, I was raging and weeping, I was yelling, my fists balled, spit flying out my mouth, and tears burning on my cheeks. I was losing it. Control was gone, its shred barely containing what little sanity I had left.

The old man nodded. He bent down and picked up my pistol. Tucking it in his pocket he tossed me his rifle. I caught it by reflex, and broke it open. There was a single .50 in the breech, and the strange weapon broke open like an old shotgun, or British range rifle. I was dumbfounded.

"What the hell do you hunt with this?"

The old man tossed me the cartridge belt around his neck, nine rods of brass hung in groups of three down its length, with pockets of gear between them. Not having a better idea, I dropped the odd baldric over my shoulder. It fit naturally, balanced by the knife that now slapped against my hip.

The old man chuckled unconcerned. "Giants mostly. Bears if they get uppity, and wolves only when I have to. There are some on my mountain boy, don't take any shit from them, but don't start anything either, I have to live here."

"Now there is a widow woman down in the town what gets lonely before church. I think she just can't abide having nothing to confess. I aim to head down the town and spend the next night or two giving her all sorts of things to repent. I figure I wouldn't mind getting a little target practice with this little toy while she cooks. Why don't you take my weapon, and take my cabin while you get your head straight? When I am done, I will leave your pistol in your truck."

I thought about the cost of those big .50's and realized this stranger was leaving me a weapon that probably cost as much as my truck.

Hell, the ammo alone could pay for filling my tank. "Sir, this is way too expensive to shoot compared to the pistol—"probably a stupid thing to say, but I was a little unsettled.

He laughed, and ravens took up the refrain from the surrounding trees.

"Ammo for her is cheap as stones, boy, she never misses. Thing is, each weapon has a nature. That is a hero's weapon. It was meant to course the deep woods, to run the high lonely places in the hands of someone lost in the hunt, who hears only the thunder of the blood, lost in the rage, lost in the purity of the moment. In the center of that storm, that weapon speaks, and when it does, you listen boy. You listen good."

Something in his words caught me, I could see myself running through the woods, the rifle held loose at its balance point like some great spear. I could feel the hammer of my blood, the rage I had been controlling suddenly, gloriously free. It was like a drug. I stood there lost in the vision, unable to think clearly. I barely heard his next words.

"Got to go, widow's waiting. It's a good thing I am taking your toy. Some weapons just have no idea what direction they are supposed to be pointing. Young guns and young men both make mistakes sometimes."

He got into an odd eight wheeled ATV and howled off down the mountain, laughing as he crashed from rock and tree in a journey down the mountain that was as much a controlled crash as drive.

He was right though, I needed some time on the mountain. I guessed I had better find that cabin first. As I headed up the mountain, I began to think. Walking with the rifle in my hands, the old patterns came back, the old senses, the old joy. My senses started to extend, started to open outward, and inward.

The silence of the wood seeped into my bones, into my soul. The forest isn't silent, there is sound in it, but between the sounds, there is a silence that speaks as well, if you can hear it. Water, stone and tree, bird and squirrel, first I heard. There were deer, I could hear them, sometimes surprisingly graceless in the woods.

There was bear sign everywhere, he wasn't kidding. There was a young mother and two cubs. They were moving through the woods as I was. I would watch for them. I saw what looked like a coyote or wolf a couple of times, just a flash of grey, swiftly gone.

I found the cabin, and stowed my gear from my "go bag". An old soldier's reflex; my vehicle always has my "go bag" or zero notice deployment essentials. One day worth of battle goodies. Survival kit, or screw-it-I'm-off-to-a-cabin-in-the-woods-kit; either way, it had rain gear, water purifiers, hydropack, paracord, knife, survival blanket, energy bars, and lighter.

I put on the hydropack, picked up the rifle and began to walk. I was alone up here with my thoughts. I wanted so bad to be home, but I was screwing it up. I gave everything to defend hearth and home, but it looked like I was the danger to them now that I was back. I grew angry, and let it run over me. I snarled, and let the rage fill me. I began to jog. The flickers of silver were back in the woods, the wolf or coyote was paralleling me again. Screw him, these were MY woods now. I pushed it harder, my breath coming faster, I flowed through the forest, my senses pushing outward, my feet seeming to find purchase on mossy rock or exposed root, never slipping, as we coursed through the forrest. Ravens cawed warning as I came, let them, they flitted through the woods after me. Did they smell the blood in my mind? Did they know what they followed?

All the bullshit welled up in me until I felt like I would be sick. All the frustration, the fear, the not knowing what I was supposed to be. It was killing me. I didn't care anymore. I snarled my rage, but joy as well. I was done being anyone. I threw off my humanity like a rotted old rag, and threw myself into the rage. I laughed as I thundered through the woods. As fast as I came, I was more quiet than the deer I passed below, and came upon the mother bear and cubs by surprise. She rose and snarled and my rifle fell unthinking on her chest, but I did not fire; I laughed and ran on, and she dropped down and moved to keep between her cubs and I. One killer to another, I thought her wise to do so.

I topped the next rise and saw a moose, his rack was large, an old bull and proud with it. He snorted and lowered his rack and pawed the ground. Without a thought I let my charge bleed off in my next steps and fell prone behind the rifle. The bull turned as if sensing his mistake in challenging, but presented his flank, and a spear of flame and hammer of pure thunder split the twilight of the forest. I had not even known I was firing, so pure had been my concentration.

I reloaded without thought, placing the empty in the lowest of the nine leather loops to be reloaded. Keeping the rifle with me, I carved as much from the bull as I could carry, but I saw the wolf shape stalking the corners of my vision, always half behind tree or rock or bush when I turned. My rifle stayed to hand. I was wrapping the last of the meat in my spare shirt (former spare shirt, now I guess it's scrap) when the bear came.

She was lean and hungry, as were her cubs. She faced me fearlessly, for she was their defender. What was I? Killer. So was she. So would they be. Was that all I was? I cut another piece off the moose and tossed it beyond her, between the cubs, and they began to pull at either end of it, bleating like baby cows. I laughed. Backing slowly away, I left the kill to her.

My hands shook, my muscles stiffened, my thoughts cleared, but still they remained. Whatever had been in my head before was gone now. Whatever I was, I was, and was OK with it. I took what meat was mine and stalked back to the cabin. The happy caw of ravens and bleating of bear cubs followed me in the forest.

I cleaned and left the rifle, although I found on it no makers mark. It was a fine made thing, I left ten dollars rolled up in the cartridge for the round I fired. I knew it cost much to buy, and saw no loader set here in the cabin, and did not think the old man here had so much as to gift me with it without loss.

I had feared the rage, and myself. I guess it was some of that "woo-woo" stuff, the magic bits of the heathen path I needed. The gods and ancestors understood the price we pay for doing what we must, and left us tools to come back men, and healthy ones, not beasts. I guess I had to put aside my humanity for a while and remind myself the beast too could be a clean thing. What I was, I was, and was OK with it.

I found my pistol on my seat. It was empty, but there was a pie with it. I guess the widow that he saw liked the old man well enough. He was a likely rogue, and if he knew women the way he seemed to know fighting men, he must have tales to tell. I felt bad; in all of this, I never asked his name.

May Day Magic

Fairy tales are just that at the root, tales of the Faery, of the Alfar, of the magical twilight world or Alfheim that is said to border our own. Where the alfs are immortal, unchanging, and magical, mankind burns sun-bright for a few heartbeats and then fades. We shine with a brightness they can never know for a short span and then are gone. We live with a fierceness that their own eternity cannot contain.

Fairy tales breathe wonder back into the world, evoke the magic of the wild places, and call to the part of us that still lives in the shadows of the great trees, and feels the seasons turn in our bones. They represent beauty, wildness, magic and wonder for us. More than human passion, lacking all human restraint, yet for all we share, they are utterly inhuman, bound by their singular nature to rules that are not our own. Fairy tales were not simply entertainment, not simply breathing wonder into the ancient world, they were a very careful manual about how to treat with the fairy and come away with your freedom and sanity.

Do not take food or drink, lest you be bound to them. Do not sleep under the hill, lest you emerge decades later. Do not take a gift from them without matching gift in return or be bound to them. Know they can never speak a lie, but they will trick you with the truth you want to hear in their words. Fairy tales used to be warnings to their listeners. Somewhere along the line we stopped teaching people the rules of an ancient game they may end up playing, should they dance the wrong way at twilight, follow a silver stag into the woods, or offer unwise oaths at fairy rings.

"Damn all women anyway," he snarled as he stumbled into the twilight of the first of May. He stopped at the forest edge and howled out his youthful pain to the listening woods: "Screw women, screw springtime, and SCREW LOVE!"

This is the story of young Andrew McLain: of oaths taken at twilight, faery dating, sacrifice, and the healing power of love.

Andrew loved Jenny with all of his heart and most of his lower regions. Jenny liked Andrew, but had been known to be fond of Kurt, and his lower regions as well. On this fine May Day, Andrew called upon Jenny with a ring, only to discover Jenny taking Kurt for a vigorous canter across the sofa.

Opening the bottle of champagne he had brought, he poured it into a ring of mushrooms at the base of an old oak, muttering, "This was supposed to toast our love, but now there's not a woman born I'd share it with." With a cry he hurled the diamond ring into the woodland stream, screaming, "Take that, love, and screw you too. I say screw every inhuman one of you".

Dangerous words already on a Mayday evening, made worse by how he ended it. . .

"Gods, I'd rather die than love again. Let love just take the heart she ruined anyway."

There are strange things that lurk in the forest deeps. There are things that walk the borders between the night and day, things ancient and inhuman, just listening and ever so hungry. There are two powers that even gods must bow to: love and fate. This is a story of both.

Andrew stomped his way into the campus forest, kicking mushrooms and ferns as he passed. Little noting the sun dipping below the horizon, he stalked into the Mayday night, into the dark primeval forest, and another age. On certain days, when the world hangs between dark and night, between the seen and unseen, the hills open, and the paths to Alfheim open again. In the dark of Yule the knights of the wild hunt ride behind the coursing wolves of the Allfather, but in the wild night of Mayday, on Walpurgsnight, it is Freya who leads the ladies of the elven court in a wild hunt of passion, the stuff of dream and nightmare.

Andrew stopped and turned, aware at last that something was amiss. He heard a sound like sirens in the near distance. Not quite sirens, not like trumpets, more like the conch shells he had heard in Hawaii. The sound came again, this time with the baying of hounds and the faint strains of laughter. It sounded like the fox hunts you saw in some old movies, but what was it doing in the University forest?

With a start, Andrew saw a dozen slim silver steeds with belled and richly tooled harnesses sweep into the clearing. Gowned ladies of eerie beauty and cold perfection sat easily in split skirts in high saddles with lances sheathed by the right knee. Inhumanly cold beauty stared at him from all sides, cold white faces and bloodless lips in a smile that could teach a cat cruelty, and eyes that burned with smouldering passion.

"Look!" rang a voice like a silver bell. "The night's stag!"

While slim white hounds circled him, Andrew protested he was no stag but a man. Each denial made the perfect inhuman beauties smile wider. Finally, surrounded by stags and mounted ladies with drawn lances, a final figure rode astride the neck of a golden boar the size of a rhino. More beautiful than the pale elfin beauties, this woman burned like fire in the night. Shining white skin, with a golden necklace burning bright in the hollow of her half-bared breasts, her laughter rang like birdsong at dawn, and her smile brought a stammering blush to Andrew's angry features.

"Now then, young man," purred the golden woman with a sensuous smile. "You poured out an offering at the Faery ring, and threw a golden offering in my sacred waters, and made strong oaths before us. You summoned my ladies on my holy night, you promised to screw my women, to screw the springtime, and to screw love."

Laughter rang from the inhuman beauties around him, and set the hounds to snarling again.

"My women ride, the spring is newborn and hungry this evening, and I am love. If you would play stag in these woods, little man, you will need more than rage. You will need Hoof and Horn!"

Her voice echoed strangely and the women began circling and chanting "Hoof and Horn, hunt till the morn." Over and over they chanted and circled until Andrew fell down, confused and burning. His hands and feet merged into a stag's split hooves, and proud antlers sprang from his brow. With a shout ,Andrew sprang from the circle and burst down the trail, desperately fleeing the spears of the women, and fangs of the hounds.

On through the forest Andrew bounded, his muscles bunching and stretching with effortless power. All the rage of frustrated love burned within him, and he fed on the thunder of his blood, growing in power and rage with every bound. Soon his pride and power could not abide the chasing hounds, and he spun at bay. Flicking his antlers left and right, he smashed two hounds against the looming trees, and spun with his hoof to catch the hamstringing third. He charged among the hounds with the fury of his frustration and humiliation, reclaiming his manhood in fury and blood. At last he stood at bay in the clearing, the living hounds slinking behind their mistresses.

"The stag is come!" shouted the golden goddess on her gleaming boar. "Come to me!" she called, throwing off her cloak and shining in naked glory before him.

Maddened with rage and lust, Andrew lunged. In a cat-like move, the boar danced aside, and Andrew's proud antlers became stuck in the tree, with his legs raised in the air in his aborted lunge at the naked rider.

One by one the circling ladies cut at him shallowly with their lances as they passed. Roaring his rage, Andrew wept, once again tricked and humiliated by women, he waited for the final thrust that would end his pain.

One by one the maidens slipped from their gowns and from their horses. Trailing fingers in the wounds they dealt him, they stroked his strong thighs and heaving chest. With burning kisses and lightning touches they transformed and enflamed him until he stood, a naked man, blooded but unwounded, crowned with a proud stags crown.

Down they pulled him to the earth, and the golden goddess brought him low with a single kiss. She whispered to his fevered ears in tones of honeyed fire.

"Love is death and rebirth, love is pain and healing, love is forgetting and forgiving, love is my gift and my worship both."

With a cry she mounted him, with a cry he answered. With laughing maidens kissing and caressing, he did a stag's duty, and knew a man's healing. As the night ended, and twilight again lit the trees, Andrew cried at last, and let go his rage. He whispered her name softly, and she smiled.

Freya stood with her elfin maids, and looked down at her lover, her prey, and smiled.

"You will know a long hunt, my stag, before you find your mate.

Run you as hard for her as you ran from me, you may yet find her. Fight half as hard to get her as to flee me, and you may win her. Love her just as fiercely as me, and you will please her."

Dawn found Andrew by the Faery ring. He looked down on the champagne bottle thrown to the ground. He picked it up. On his hands and knees, he removed the cork and wire, and other bits of garbage. Backing away, he bowed awkwardly. With a smile he turned and walked into the future, whistling a love song.

The Nom-Nom Gnome

Change is something that so far I have spoken of only in terms of people. In fact, the truth of any relationship that is real and healthy is that It is reciprocal. We speak of our relationships with each other, with the wights of the lands and waters, with the spirits of our ancestors, and with the gods as being reciprocal gifting relationships. We treat as equals, by the getting judging the giving, that what we build are connections and not debts between each other.

We do not exist in a vacuum. We are each of us connected, from the first primodial ancestor to the least of the children yet unborn through the web of wyrd. Web is not rope, it does not stretch simply back in time and forward, but connects us to those beside and around us, encompassing our whole world, seen and unseen.

By seen and unseen I speak less of the esoteric and more of the unnoticed. Our ancestors lived intimately with the land and its cycles. The health and wellbeing of the folk was tied inexorably and unquestionably with the health of the forest, field, flock, stream and sea. There was no question that as the land prospered, so did we, as it failed, so we came to peril, famine, and disaster.

While our ancestors might call upon the gods on high feast days or at war, the proper place of the gods was in communal worship, the good of the tribe, village or people. Most of our lives are really not that grand in scope, nor require such distant and awesomely powerful forces. Most of our daily lives are quite pedestrian, and our needs quite small in scope, quite personal and real in consequence.

For this reason, our ancestors' daily practice spent much time on the ancestors, who could be taken as having both an intimate understanding of our problems, and a stake in our success or failure. There was one other group that loomed far larger in ancestral practice than it does for many modern humans; the wights.

Size matters, as does distance. The wights of the mountain are vast, ancient, and powerful. We can build a relationship with the jötun of the mountains, but the primal forces that drive them are true to their nature, as they must be, and when they are drawn to move and act, it will be in accordance with that nature.

Those great wights are not the only ones we share the world with, nor indeed the closest. When I spoke of the seen and unseen, I should perhaps have phrased it the noticed and unnoticed, for the most important of wights we often do not notice, or do not notice in the context of wights.

A wight is a spirit; some have bodies, some do not, some have places instead of bodies. The wights of field, forest and farm were known well to our ancestors, and to those whose way of life ties them to the land today. In an urban culture, that includes few indeed among the folk, but the ties that bind us to the land and to the world are not so easily broken, nor the wights so easily left behind.

You cannot take the flocks from the folk entire, those whom the herd-lord hears are called ever to their care, even in an apartment that could pass for a jail cell, even if it costs more than a ranch in more spacious settings. There are still the house wights.

What are house wights? The hearth spirit, the central spirit of a house, a place,that receives some of the energy of all that transpires in that place, a genius loci. What we do changes the spirit of a place. A house of warmth and love will become a wellspring of comfort and rest, able to return the gift for a gift by giving back that energy when your strength is low, your mind or mood dark, hurt, or troubled. A house of strife and anger will take up that energy too, and the wights themselves will darken. Like any who have learned to hate, they too will wait until your mind or mood is dark, your strength low, and give you a nudge farther into darkness and not out of it. We speak of the web of wyrd because we are born into a world that is not our making, and leave a world to others that has been changed by us. We change the world with every breath, every choice, every action. We change the land by our actions as much as we change ourselves. The difference with Heathens is we actually understand this, and can consciously seek to strengthen those relationships that they be positive and healthy.

We do not have rats infesting our communal grain storage in the hut, yet we have more cats than ever. We do not have sheep or cattle in the carpark, yet we have dogs sleeping at our door where none have seen a wolf in fifty years. We fill our window boxes with flowers, our corners with potted plants in decorative hangers. People lavish care and talk to these wights of the house, giving the gifts of love and duty, of welcome. Lastly, we have the garden gnome.

Ah, the garden gnome. The house wight statue, the protector of the garden, the only pagan statue you will see receiving offerings the ancients would have understood even in the front gardens of your local churches. The garden gnome is a symbol and reminder of our house wights. Unlike a *mountain, a garden gnome is not vast and unchanging, it is small and close, and the reciprocal gifting relationship we have (whether we are conscious of it or not) can and will change its nature, even as our own nature changes by those same choices and actions. Our relationship is intimate, for all that is often unnoticed.*

The Sto:Lo tribes would pass through, but never stay. They feared the spirit of this place, calling it a Basket Ogre. Its fearsome shape, peering out of the trees like a child-devouring monster, would give them no peace. Each season one tribe or another would come to hunt and fish, but never to stay.

When the Europeans came, the demon-haunted trees scared the churchgoing town folk, but the hardy pioneers and hill folk were of stronger stuff. With stout axes and saws, they cleared the land for planting. With few tools and fewer animals, they tamed the wild spirits of the land, and with the blood and sweat they poured into the soil, they made it their own.

Few of the great wild wights and svartly elves lingered in the dark places of the forest, still resisting the axes and saws of man, the iron ribbons of his railroads, the stone rivers of his roads. The Basket Ogre would not yield. When its rock was shattered by the railway men, it moved into a young sapling. Year upon year it sunk its roots deep, waiting and hating, until one year in the heavy rains it held the runoff deep within the soil until half the hillside slipped down into the river, carrying the hated railroad and brickworks right into the river. The town rebuilt away from the haunted place, and the Basket Ogre waited in its twisted tree, and hated some more.

Lars and Betty Olson came west to the mountains, seeking a new beginning. Lars had fought in the Second World War, and when he returned, wanted to start a family in a simpler life, away from the madness he had seen. To claim and clear the ill-omened land seemed a good way for a young family to make a place in this half-tamed land. A lone maple tree, heavy and twisted, loomed about the place, seeming to threaten the little firs and cedars of the rest of the woods. Lars laughed: the town was called Haney, but from the way that old man kings it on the hill, it might be called Maple Ridge (as indeed it one day would). Betty hated the tree, and asked Lars to cut it down. Lars looked at the tree, and felt its black hatred. It made him laugh. It's a nasty old bugger, just like me, he would say.

As often happens with young couples, children came along in time, and soon beneath that old maple grew a small horde of small, then not so small children. The little house grew, and the yard grew fences and outbuildings, and everywhere were the signs of children, mischief and fun, everywhere except the old maple. Only Lars would go and sit with his drink, and talk, as he said, one nasty old bugger to another.

In summer time, the house would ring again with the thunder of little feet, the laughter of little voices, as the first lot of grandchildren would come to stay. Among the children was Betty's delight, young Iris. Iris was a happy child, but one who saw things that others missed, or at least said things that others only thought. When she saw her grampa trip over the root of the big ugly maple in the back yard, her eyes grew very big.

"Grampa," she said, "When you tripped, I saw a big face with great big teeth growling at you from the tree."

Lars laughed, and rubbed her head. "That would be the ugly little alf in the tree. I swear he'd love to gobble you up." He made a little mouth with his outstretched hands and chased and tickled her around, making "Nom-nom-nom" biting sounds as he nibbled at her hair with his pretend jaws.

When the grandchildren asked later about the mean alf in the tree, Grandpa Lars had to tell them all about the legends of wights and alfar, and how they were remembered here with the little garden gnomes people put out for their house-wights to live in. Iris declared

94

that the Nom-Nom alf in the tree was mean because he had such an ugly tree to live in, causing Grandma Betty to laugh, as she had heard some of the local lore about the mean old thing.

When Yuletide came, and the grandchildren came for dinner and presents, grandma and grandpa got a surprise. Besides the presents for each of them, there was the strangest gift they had ever seen. A ceramic garden gnome, with a big goofy smile, and terrible shining teeth. It was ugly, cheerful, a happy little monster painted in bright, slightly sloppy colours. Iris announced that she had made it for the Nom-Nom Gnome, so he could have someplace nicer to live. Grandpa Lars thought it the funniest thing, and decided they should put on coats and boots, and head out into the snow to introduce the Nom-Nom Gnome to his new home. Explaining to the other children how important it was to bring a little bit of the feast to share with the Nom-Nom Gnome to make it feel welcome, he tore off a bit of ham, and clutched it with his wine as he stomped off through the snow towards the waiting tree. A procession of slightly drunk and amused adults, mixed with slightly frightened but excited children, followed the solemn Iris and her bright painted gnome.

He was the Basket Ogre, the terror of children. He had terrified the bravest Sto:Lo warriors, caused the great shaman to stay away from the lands he haunted, and this was the Yule-tide, the heart of the dark, the height of his power. The grey one came with them, the old warrior. Such fear he had faced in his life, such hatred he had fought and overcome that the Basket Ogre had no power over him. He had watched the railroad men come, and swept the work of decades into the river with his power; he had driven off the pioneers, terrified the wild trappers and lumbermen; what could he fear from little children? Wise as the old alf was, he did not know the lore of the north and the magic hidden in the laws of hospitality.

Iris held up the painted statue, a garden gnome, painted in bright happy colours, yet with fierce and terrible fangs. "Happy Yule to you Nom-Nom Gnome, here is your new home" She planted the gnome at the base of the tree, looking towards the house.

Lars put a slice of ham in the snow in front of it, and poured wine from his glass to spill across the rough bark and red hat of the gnome. "Share meat and drink from our table, be our guest at our feasts as we have been guests on your land. Be welcome in our home, little gnome."

One after the other, the adults and children left a gift and a smile for the Nom-Nom Gnome, and turned back from the wind to the hall and the home. The ogre slipped gently from root to the gnome, feeling the warmth and the welcome in the painted old stone. Hate and pain are hard habits to break, but hospitality is magic both subtle and strong, for the Ogre felt powerfully drawn to the gnome. Long he had hated, feared and alone. Now he was welcomed and offered a home. In the heart of his power, in the dark and the cold, the Ogre felt oddly lost and alone. Land takings have power, hospitality builds bonds, the magic of Yuletide is both quiet and strong. Gifts freely given of welcome and love can make greater change than a bolt from above.

Summer is coming and the children return; the Ogre is watching to see what will come. Iris brings a blanket, and wagon behind. She picked up the Nom-Nom Gnome, and went for a ride. She took him around to the old patio, and with her girl cousins had high tea with scones. The boys in their turn took the fierce painted gnome, set him up as the king and then played at war. With girls he had feasting, with boys played at war, until the anger of ogres wasn't his anymore.

Lars passed away, and was laid beneath the tree. The Gnome was the marker the family could see. Betty alone found the place hard to keep. Deep in the stone of the old battered gnome woke the fierceness of ogres to defend his new home. With the power of a svart alf he warded the home, slaughtering aphids to defend the roses, bringing the berries where old women can reach, and scaring off dogs who would poop on the lawn. Try as he might, the gnome couldn't stop time, so with the years came the day Betty died.

He who had hated so long and so hard, cursed that stone had no tears he could cry. Ogre no more but the old Nom-Nom Gnome, he silently guarded the now empty home. The day of the funeral the grandchildren came. Almost grown up now, and too old to play. Iris was crying, her bright eyes did weep. At last to the garden, an old friend to seek. He's a battered old gnome, care-worn and drab, but a piece of her childhood and link to her past.

"Nom-Nom!" She laughed, with her eyes full of tears. Just the sight of him brought back her earliest years. His paint was all faded, his fangs and his cap, but she picked him up gently and turned him around. "I can't leave you here for some stranger to own, you must come with me now, I'm taking you home."

In a teenager's room, with a fresh coat of paint, sits Nom-Nom the Gnome who forgot how to hate. Not an ogre to fear but a goodly house wight; he will keep his folk's home, and keep it all right.

Chapter 3: Death

Yule Tale

To be born is to die. Life for humans is that period that falls between birth and death. Sometimes that is a negative value for those who die in the womb without ever tasting a single breath of life. The rest of us know a span of indeterminate length between birth and death in which we have a chance to build worth through our deeds, to learn about this world, to sing, dance, laugh, play, build, strive, struggle, lose, hurt, heal, learn and repeat; but only for a time. To Wyrd even the gods must bow, for all things that have a beginning have an ending. Accepting that you will, and indeed must die does not mean lying down and accepting death without struggle. Death is the end of all things, the good and the bad, the laughter and the pain, but mostly it is the death of possibilities, for as long as you have life, you may change things. The wise do not quibble with the coming of death so much as they dicker about the date for the appointment.

At the Yuletide we come together as a people, we wassail hard to let hospitality and cheer burn bright in the heart of the dark. We brighten each other with gifts, and renew the ties that bind us, each to the other at Yule because our ancestors understood this simple truth; at the Yuletide, in the heart of the dark, life hangs by a thread, and death and the dead are a heartbeat away. The veil between the worlds of the living and the dead fades with the sun, and at Yule the veil is thin enough that those who are near to passing are often drawn to cross.

Present: Dec 21, Canada

Grandpa McKay was in fine form. Since Grandma passed away at New Year's last year, Grandpa had been letting his diet slide, and worrying a lot less about the little things like civilization, propriety, and the expectations of his children.

He gave out his gifts to the kids with strict instructions that they should open them here, and then go read the first page in their rooms. His son and daughter in law looked over with resignation as their 14 year old daughter and 12 year old son unwrapped a hardcover Nancy Drew and Hardy-boy mystery. The kids rolled their eyes, but their daughter caught grandpa's wink and head gesture towards their room, and decided that sneak grandpa was without adult supervision since grandma passed away, and maybe they should REALLY look at them in her room.

"Thanks, Grandpa!" Caitlyn said lightly as she grabbed her brother by his hoodie and dragged him off. "Say thanks, Karl," she muttered as she dragged her younger brother off.

"You know papa, I think the kids are a little old for those books. I mean, I got those when I was eight, and they were pretty old then," said his daughter-in-law Christine.

"I'm old," Grandpa said with a wicked twinkle. "If I don't use that excuse to get away with stuff, what's the point?" he laughed.

In their room, Caitlyn opened up her book and found a prepaid iTtunes card for $100, while Karl found his pre-paid gaming card for the same amount. Eyes burning with sheer honest youthful greed, they shared a flashing smile, and said together, "Grandpa's cool!"

Christine had been raised a good Christian, but living with a heathen husband had pretty much confused the issue for her to the point that she had even begun cursing to both pantheons when stubbing her toe or dropping something. The kids were agnostic about most things, but held as a simple fact of existence that Easter and Yule family traditions were not so much holy as a central pillar of their universe, which has always been so, and would always remain so.

At the beginning of the feast, Grandpa took a plate, took a slice of ham, and went around the table to get a piece of something from everyone to offer to the wights. When Karl stabbed a hated Brussels sprout to get rid of, he looked in grandpa's eyes, and remembered why they were giving. With a painful sigh, he took some of his triple helping of mashed potatoes and cheese sauce and added it to the plate. James poured a tall glass of mead and followed his father out to the old battered gnome (Nom-Nom) that lived in the front garden, and stood as focus for the families' offerings. As his father bent slowly and painfully (James didn't like to think about how much frailer his father was since his mother's passing) to leave the offering plate, he poured out the mead on the snow before the gnome.

"Hail the wights and spirits of this place, hail the holy gods at this Yuletide. Mead from our home, and welcome from our hearth is yours!"

Grandpa spoke:

"Hail the fallen, those who are in our hearts, but not our halls. From the mound we call you, sing your praise, and set your place at the feast. Be welcome in our halls, as forever you are in our hearts."

He said the words they had heard a hundred times before, but there was a weight to them that caught everyone, and Christine grabbed her husband's arm and they shared a worried look.

Grandpa rose, and his knees gave a great crack.

"Mother-Friker!" he cursed "Cheap fuggin' army replacement kneecap!" he swore, breaking the spell.

"Grandpa!" laughed the children in mock horror, amused at his cursing. They returned to the feast.

Inside, after the feast, when the egg nog and desserts were broken out, Christine chided her father in law when he asked for rum for his egg nog. "Grandpa," she said, "you know Grandma said you can't have alcohol with your medication, it's bad for your heart."

Grandpa's voice got distant, and he looked into a distance that only he could see.

"Grandma's dead. A whole lot of my friends are dead. I lift my glass these days to those I love, and you here in this room are the only living names I call. Yule is the heart of the dark, the height of the cold. The veil between the dead and us grows thin, we can hear them, and they can hear us. They call to me, and one day soon I shall answer."

He silenced their protests with a gesture that owed more to sergeant's stripes than parenthood, and his voice grew stronger.

"Cattle die, kinsmen die
You too will die
One thing alone will not die
The fame of a good man's deeds

I am not so afraid of death, as that I will stop living. This is Yule, I am alive. I feast, I revel, eat too much, drink too much, and fart as loudly as possible." The adults rolled their eyes as he waggled his bushy eyebrows, but the children giggled.

"I should have died long ago, but I had things to do, and wouldn't go. My body is failing, and I have the choice between cowering for

100

a decade from anything enjoyable, and dying alone in my own crap like a baby who doesn't even know its name, or getting shot by a jealous husband sneaking out of some woman's bedroom. I know which one I'm picking."

As the night wore on, Caitlyn and Karl snuck the rum and spiked grandpa's egg nog with a mischievous grin. They exchanged the winks of the wicked in a house where parental concern was the common foe.

When they dropped him at his door, he was unwilling to face his empty house, and strode instead to the pub at the end of the walk. Yule was upon him, and memory with it. The dead were with him, and would not let him go. All feast he remembered his dear wife Adrianne, the long suffering woman who put up with his endless deployments, the moves, the moods and the silences when he was between them. That she died first surprised the both of them, for his time was borrowed since the war.

Past: 25 March, Kiseljak, Bosnia-Herzegovina

"Better call it in, Sparks," Master Corporal Ternapolski muttered to his radioman.

Signalman McKay picked up the mic from his field radio and began to call in the confirmation of Bosnian regular armed forces backing irregulars in attacks on Croat civilians. It had been known and denied for some time, known by the troops and locals, denied by the leaders on all sides, that the Bosnian regulars were backing the long string of regrettable incidents happening to anyone of the wrong race when Bosnia-Herzegovnia settled its ethnic question. Reports from witnesses are easily dismissed; reports from UN troops with direct observations are not. The Bosnians were good at not getting caught, so the Royal Canadian Regiment, 2nd Battalion, made a big noise about setting up checkpoints, and quietly sent out probing forces along all the bypass routes to find out what people were doing when the Canadians supposedly couldn't see them. It was against some interpretations of the rules, but General MacKenzie was known to stretch rules like cheap elastics to get the job done.

After a few minutes the word came back to show themselves, in order to force the Bosnians to withdraw their regulars or admit they were behind the massacres. Ternapolski looked at his radio man and said, "Lets get the Iltis. If this goes badly, I want to be able to get out of there before someone does anything stupid."

They crested the hill, their blue helmets and UN pennon flapping as the two tanks, half-dozen APCs, and dozens of trucks gathered about the crossroads began to swarm with activity. There was shouting from one of the civilian-clad armed men, and the 14.5mm machine gun on one of the Bosnian APCs began to fire at the Canadian Iltis.

"Call it in! Call it in!" screamed out Ternapolski, as his German accent came out. He pulled the light all-terrain vehicle through a bouncing turn and tore off down the hill. They blazed away from the Bosnian troops, pursued by small arms fire as infantry flanking the hill shot at them.

Almost a quarter-kilometer away, as they approached the turn, their get away came to an abrupt end. Like the Hammer of Thor, a shell from the Bosnian T55 lifted their vehicle into the air, shattering its light frame, and spilling its twisted form into the ditch. The force of the blast tore Mcpl Ternapolski partially apart, while the heavy radio partially shielded Signalman McKay. Lying dazed and battered, half under his Iltis in the rocky ditch beside the cross roads McKay saw something he would later tell his son about when very, very drunk. Something he knew was real, and knew couldn't be.

His ears ringing, and a muffled sobbing coming from someplace (probably him), McKay felt along his combats, to feel the jagged bone of one of his ribs actually jutting through his battle-dress. It was a killing wound, anyone could see that. To prove the point, two ravens lit upon the ground and began to eye him speculatively.

"I can't die, you know, " he said conversationally to the ravens. "Adrianne has agreed to marry me, which is good, because I'm pretty sure she's pregnant. I promised her that she wouldn't have to face it alone if we got pregnant, so you see, I can't die, I have to go home."

A laugh greeted those words. He looked towards the laugh and saw combat boots bloused into Canadian Forces ODs—olive drab battledress. As the feet and the attached legs moved closer, he noticed that the ODs were filled out really well by a woman who was boldly striding across the crossroads, apparently unconcerned at the slamming, somewhat inaccurate, fire coming from the two tanks in the distance.

"You are coming with me," she said, bending down to show a face tanned and lined by one who works in the sun, with eyes like glacial ice, and the smile of one who firmly expects to win every argument, and is happy to prove it.

Something about her uniform was bothering him. But hanging upside down, holding his guts in place, he decided to think about it later, and just answered with the first thing that popped in his head.

"Not unless you buy me a drink first, and clear it with my wife."

The blonde threw her head back and laughed, exposing a name tag that seemed to swim between saying Sigrun and being indecipherable runes. Where her Canadian Flags should be were black raven patches. Confused by the inconsistencies, he saw her reach in and pull him from under the vehicle and prop him up.

"My father told me a long time ago that no soldier worth his salt will turn down a pretty girl who wants to take him home. And I want to take you home. Besides, there is work to be done, and you are needed."

Gagging from the pain of being moved, and with rage at his commitment to his wife-to-be being questioned balancing the injury-given urge to pass out, McKay choked out a rebuttal.

"Then your father's a prick! I promised my fiancée I would be true, that I would return, that she would not raise our children alone. I am no oath breaker!"

The woman knelt, and looked long and hard into his fury filled eyes, and squinted. Behind her the two ravens croaked and hissed at each other with some passion, before flitting away to a nearby tree to watch. Smiling a little secret smile, she spoke very softly.

"My father doesn't like oath breakers. Your wound should take you. You will never heal from it, and you will carry its weight as long as you live. Are you strong enough?"

Seeing his snarling grin, she laughed again, this time light and relaxed.

"If you bear it long enough, and keep your oaths, I will buy you that drink. And mother says you are right about father."

With a casual sway she sauntered out of sight, and the sound of aircraft screaming overhead let him know that he had help on the way. He closed his eyes to rest. He could bear it, he had things to do.

Recovery vehicles would be along for the broken. The army was too poor to waste even the mostly broken men or machines, so what could be pieced back together would be back in service before the end of mission. Life goes on.

Present, Dec 21, Canada

Old Man McKay stomped into the bar, and hung his coat on the corner of the booth. He lowered himself into the cushions, and allowed a sigh to escape his lips. It was hard. Every day he got a little older, and the pain got a little stronger. With Adrianne gone, he found he got angry faster, slept almost never, and was tired all the time. Still, life was good. He laughed. His grandchildren were going to give his son a fine white beard like his soon. Good! Children need strong spirits to be worth a damn in this life.

He was watching the waitress walk towards his table, admiring the curves with the uncomplicated joy of a man who knows what he likes and could care less if anyone notices, when his attention was taken by the opening of the door.

The door was opened by a Captain from his old Regiment. Wearing the Dress Greens of 2nd Batallion, Royal Canadian Regiment, Airborne Company, a tall muscular blonde woman stalked into the bar like a lioness into a sheep pen. Tucking her cap casually under one arm, she grinned as she approached his table.

"I owe you a drink. I am here to collect."

The last word rang like the sound of a closing breech-block, and he looked into the face he last saw many years ago, when he nearly died with his best friend. Nodding to the waitress, she called for a bottle of scotch, the good stuff from under the shelf. She passed along a stack of bills and told her to be quick.

McKay looked at Sigrun, this time knowing the name and the runes that spelled it. His mouth was dry, but it wasn't in an old man to fear anything. This was Yule, and the veil between the living and the dead was thin; the hunt rode the night, the dead walked, and why should a chooser of the slain not keep a date so long deferred? He grinned. No need to watch the diet tonight, after all.

The bottle arrived and the waitress made to leave glasses, but the Captain shooed her away.

"Off with you, child, this is soldiers' business. Serious drinking."

Handing the bottle to McKay with an almost ceremonial gesture, she watched him raise it to the sky.

"To the Æsir!" He took a strong pull of the fiery liquid, feeling it settle warmth into the corners of his soul. Handing the bottle over with hands still stiff from the cold, he was unsurprised when she raised the bottle high and answered with a voice that would be at home on any parade square or battle field.

"To the Vanir!" Her throat worked as she took a long pull of the bottle. She had a wide, uncomplicated smile on her face as she continued, as she handed the bottle back.

"Twenty-three years old, this scotch; same as you, the last time we met."

Unwilling to show any weakness at the end, or before a woman as beautiful as this, he matched her aplomb with the last toast.

"TO THE FALLEN!" he took a long burning swallow, feeling the fire inside. Tears streamed down his face, as he let the memories come back, one and all.

"Master Corporal John Ternapolski," he said, naming his dead friend.

She raised the bottle in return and named another, and another. One sip per soul, they killed the bottle remembering the dead. At last the bottle was all but empty, and she took it back one last time.

"I bought you a drink. But I bring something else. Your wife sends a message. It is time to come home. You are needed, soldier. I have come to collect."

They rose together, and stalked out. He moved lightly, and sure, as if his knee no longer pained him, as if his ribs and hip were no longer scars and fragments. As she opened the door, he saw an army staff car waiting. As the driver opened the door, McKay was unsurprised to see Mcpl Ternapolski holding the door.

"Man, you got fat, Sparks," quipped his dead friend.

"Hope you drive better than last time," McKay replied.

As Sigrun settled into the car beside him, McKay heard the waitress scream inside. "Oh my god, the old man is dead!"

McKay smiled. His last Yule had been a good one.

Yule is the heart of the dark, the killing cold, the dying time. At this time, we will lose loved ones. At this time of loss and darkness, it is easy to draw away, and forget the ones who have passed, to draw away from the ones you fear to lose next. Do not.

Yule is the time when the dead and the living are nearest. Yule is the time for the renewing of bonds, the strengthening of ties between this generation and the next, between those who went before, and those who will come after.

Remember those who you have, and let them know how much you care. Remember those you have lost, and make bright the memories of laughter, life and struggle that you shared. Wassail hard in the heart of the dark, for only this will keep alive the light.

Take strength from the love of those you have known, take solace in those who touched your life, however briefly. Reach out to old friends, and to new ones. In the light, it is easy to see who is with you. In the dark, you must reach out to know, and to be known. In the dark, we are only alone if we forget. In the dark, we embrace pain, for the memory of love.

Noir

Mankind has always gathered around the fire to tell ghost stories. A part of us is as unwilling to let our dead go as are dead are to let go the world. As much as we struggle to understand and accept death in our lives, the idea of a ghost comes from the unwillingness of the dead to accept the things that happened in life.

The heathens understand the reason that Hel has two faces, for death is both beautiful and terrible. Hel is the unbroken promise, the silence at the end of song, an end to pain, a welcome home at the end of the longest journey. Hel does not cut our threads; wyrd weaves as it will, and Hel has no more need to hunt the living than gravity to hunt birds. To the grave all life will come in time, as every bird at last to earth. The dead are hers, and she keeps them well. To those suffering and in pain, those whom life has worn thin and wan, her face shines the warm beauty of a maiden, the colour of mercy and an end to suffering. To those who have yet to live fully, or who see from their lives a loved one torn, her face is corpse bloated horror, the grim specter of loss incarnate.

There are those who will not accept the grave, those whose sense of duty will not end with their lives. The Einherjar. The valliant dead. Our ancestors understood these souls, those who would never be free of the struggles they not only endured in life, but became forever wed to. The halls of Folkvangr and Valhalla ring with the songs of the Einherjar in myth and legend, Freya goddess of love and war both taking half of the eternal warriors, while Odin the Battle-glad and Victory Father the other half. There can be no rest for such souls, and there will be none. Their watch can never end, their duty never done, but they can learn under such tutors how to be at peace with the struggle they are bound to.

There is a human need for judgment. Christianity makes much of guilt as a tool, and forgiveness as a trade-good. Business has traditionally been brisk. For a heathen the question is one not of sin but of worth. The deeds that we do affect our worth. One problem that we have with this as human beings is that we cannot judge those deeds, and thus our worth as they may only be judged by those whose lives we touch. As a result, the worst of us

*think ourselves far greater than we merit, and the best of us carry the shame
of the failures to meet our own expectations.*

*Ghosts can be bound as much by those burdens as the living. We are all
bound together, the living, the dead, and those yet to be born. The deeds done
by our ancestors affect us deeply today, and the words and deeds we do in
this life or leave behind will have effects in others that will be felt long after
our passage. Not all of the most important deeds of our life will be seen as
such by us, for you cannot know the worth of your actions to another. Living
or dead, your worth is not fixed, as the changes you made upon the world
and the people in it carry forward. Living or dead, the world is as reluctant
to give you up as we are to let it go.*

How it began:

Soundly asleep then instantly awake, but not knowing why. The clock
reads 2:00 am; the house is silent except for the ever-present dripping
of the leaky faucet in the bathroom. 'Why am I awake?' I thought to
myself. My mind was alert to every sound and shift of shadow, my
heart beating quickly out of time but not afraid. Suddenly I realized I
wasn't alone, not that I could see anyone in the darkened room, but I
could feel a presence. . . instead of racing faster, my heartbeat calmed.
I felt strangely safe even though I knew I shouldn't. Who could be
in my house, in my room, and why wasn't I afraid? I sat up in bed
and turned on the lamp on the night stand. Looking across my room
I saw. . .

I don't know how long it had been this time. When you're dead, time doesn't matter that much. I got plugged back in '32, that was OK. You cross some lines, you have to figure there's going to be a cost. A dame gets involved and suddenly you start breaking your own rules, people get hurt. Dead hurt. I fixed it back then, but not before the kid got caught up in it. One innocent, and a whole bunch of mooks who probably had it coming. Like I did. Somebody was keeping score though, 'cause it didn't end when I died.

It was '43 when I got brought back first, I think. . . that little wop kid getting a bum rap because he had the wrong accent when they needed to hang an ugly rap that came from one of the country club set. Last time was, what, '93, the old broad who thought she was losing it because she could see me. She couldn't see her kid putting the squeeze on her loot, or selling her meds on the street.

He took a long drag on his smoke, pulling it deep into his lungs. The cherry on the end burned in the night like a red eye. Ghost smoke into ghost lungs. The broad on the bed turned and looked right at him, and turned on the light. He put out the smoke on the wall, noting it didn't leave a mark. Ghost smokes don't leave marks. Neither did he. Or at least, not enough to erase the mark he made when he was alive.

He waited for the screams to start, or looking at the bottle from last night to figure out where the ghost crawled out of. He hated this part. Funny how nobody wants to listen to the dead they called back. It's not like he chose to be here. That's a lie. He smiled, cold and hard. *I made my choice a long time ago. Every drinker knows, no matter what's your poison, the bill comes due at the end of the night. It's a long night when you're dead.*

Time to find out what this dame's story was. He didn't always get it right, sometimes they still died. He didn't know how many times he had to get it right before he would get to rest. Not a lot else to do when you're dead. She didn't seem to be screaming. Maybe this one would listen long enough to stay alive.

The spectral man seemed to be waiting for me to do something. . . perhaps scream or faint, not sure. He seemed surprised when I just watched him calmly. He looked vaguely familiar, like I should know him from somewhere. Perhaps he simply reminded me of someone I knew once or something. I took a moment to assess him. He had all the marks of a hard life when he'd been alive; at least I assumed he did. Not knowing how death worked, I really couldn't say. Part of me knew I should be freaking out or questioning my sanity, but for some reason, the only thing the spirit inspired in me was a sense of safety and calm, I knew somehow that he wasn't here to hurt me.

Perhaps it was his eyes that inspired that: they had the look of a man resigned to his fate, tinged with a touch of sadness. He put on a strong front as he drew on a spectral cigarette before putting it out against my wall. I was more than a little bit relieved to see that it didn't leave a burn mark. They were always so hard to remove— I'd learned that well enough from an ex-boyfriend who had been nothing but trouble when we were together and for a time even more trouble when we broke up. I still don't know what it was I saw in him to begin with; maybe it was the challenge of the bad boy that many women make the mistake of assuming they can change, or perhaps pure masochism on my part. Whatever it had been, it was bad from beginning to end and I was well quit of him. I decided to say something, maybe find out what he was here for. I was sure the spirit had a reason for being here; he didn't seem the type to just be wandering through randomly. It was like I knew that he had a message of some sort, or perhaps he simply needed my help.

"Um... hello?" I said, hoping that we could actually communicate.

* * *

The broad wasn't freaking out like most of them did. Wasn't just sitting there giggling like that twit in '73; she never got straight long enough from the junk she was on to realize what was up. It wasn't hard watching that one go. I watched a lot of people go in the Great War, and a few when I came back and worked as a cop. Only a few more when I started work as a private dick, but one of those was her. Angie. The one I screwed up. The reason I'm here.

This girl looked smart, he could work with that. She didn't look scared, though. That was bad. He may not have figured out much about why he kept coming back, but he knew that he only came back for kids on the edge of getting whacked. Innocents like Angie. No bottle this time, and no blonde; no chance to screw it up.

Sometimes they got in deep with the wrong people. Sometimes it was family, and that got real ugly. Sometimes it was love; God knows love is what screwed him up bad enough to let Angie get killed. Even dead, that one won't let him go.

This girl didn't have the look; didn't look hunted or scared. That was bad. She had no idea what was coming for her, and couldn't tell me. I pulled my .45 and checked the clip; five rounds, always five. It begins again the same.

The girl pulled the blanket up when I pulled my gat, but still didn't look scared. She should be. I only had one chance to get it right. Last chance was all I ever got.

Memory gets bad towards the end, the things you try not to bring with you. I remember the endings. The blonde comes again, when I lose, she spits on me. When I win she kisses me. Funny, when she kissed me for real, I lost it all. I lost Angie. The dark one comes, her I know. Half her face rotted and rat chewed, like the guys the shells dug out and tossed back in the trenches, all swollen up and bursting. Half her face pale, cold, and hard. A smile like the cocked hammer of my .45. Then the dark. Always the dark.

I walked forward into the light; no shadows for me I guess, since I'm not much more than one myself. It was time to talk. Probably too late, I was usually too late. Two rounds wasted, one bottle and one girl gone.

"What's your story kid? Who wants you dead?"

111

I lit another cigarette and took a drag. The smoke pulled deep and held as I looked for her response. Surprise. Huh. Always hard when you didn't see it coming.

"Nothing personal, toots, but if you see me, you got maybe an hour before somebody gets dead. And right now, the smart money is still on you."

I blew a long trail of smoke into the lamp light, and I laughed gently.

"But I always bet the wrong way, and sometimes win."

My smile used to do the trick. Calmed the guys in the trenches, calmed the cops on the scene who were turning green over their first corpse. It never worked on dames though. Of course, I never got that part right. Even dead.

* * *

Dead? Someone wanted me dead, and this spirit was here to warn me. The gun he'd pulled out had startled me a bit, but I still didn't think he was here to hurt me, but asking me who wanted me dead, that was totally unexpected. To the best of my knowledge no one wanted me dead. I mean the only person I could even think of who might even be angry with me was Joey, I mean he did take the break up hard and I had to get a restraining order, but I couldn't imagine him actually wanting me dead because of it. . . could I?

Well, there was no way to be sure. If this spirit was here to warn me of my impending potential death, then I had best figure out what to do about it. From the sound of things, he felt there might be a chance for me to survive, so I'd better work quickly. Did he know the nature of the threat; was it personal, could it be accidental? All I knew for sure was that I wasn't about to just sit in bed and let it happen. My mother didn't raise a fool; she made sure that if her baby girl got herself into trouble she was strong enough to get herself out of it. I nodded my understanding to the shade, and got out of bed. Moving to my dresser I started pulling clothes out, I wasn't going to face whatever was coming in my freaking nightgown. I paused only momentarily to glance at the spirit, but than continued to get dressed. He'd mentioned an hour at most; now was no time for modesty. Fully dressed in a tee shirt and jeans, I pulled my hair back into a ponytail to keep it out of my face and moved to my closet. I found myself very glad that my parents had seen fit to teach me how to shoot as I opened the gun safe and took out my 9mm Glock. For a moment I considered grabbing my father's .357 magnum, but I wanted something light, just in case. Who knew what I was going to be up against. Speed and maneuverability might be my saving grace. I made sure it was loaded with a round chambered and put a couple of extra clips in my pocket just to be sure.

I decided to grab my hiking boots and put them on. Who knew if I was going to need to make a run for it. I was still unnaturally calm through all of this; well, maybe I would fall apart later, if I made it through the rest of the night. Once again I turned to look at the spirit, harbinger of doom or saving angel, didn't matter, I was going to take full advantage of this warning. I for one was not ready to die this night.

"Okay, now what?" I asked him.

* * *

She said she didn't have a clue who would want her dead, but her eyes said she was lying. She picked up a cannon, and put it back in favor of some boxy piece that looked like someone took my .45 and squashed it down to half size. She stripped the clip and checked it, chambering and safing what looked like about a 9mm like she knew what she was doing. This dame had her head straight. I might save her, like I should have saved Angie.

"Hey toots, how about you roll up that sleeping bag in the closet, and put it under your covers like you was still asleep."

The closet was beside the door; anyone sitting in it would see the bed, but the door was out of sight. To get a shot at the bed, you would have to step around the walk-in closet, with your back to it.

"Sit yourself here in the closet. I will let you know when somebody comes through the door. If they start shooting at the bed, don't blow smoke asking stupid questions, you plug them hard and fast until they drop. If they look like they are turning to face you, plug 'em again."

The kid looked green, like it was sinking in, but she checked the safety, and worked it to make sure it broke clean. Her face went flat, like newbies' usually did, faking cool until they bought it themselves. I saw that a lot in the trenches, and on the force. Sometimes I saw it in the mirror, or the bottom of a bottle.

It must of been about twenty minutes, but the sweat off the girl showed she felt it like hours. I forget how much the waiting gets to you; when you're dead, some things just get easier.

I heard the back door open. I slipped into the hall to see a young guy pull a key from the lock. Huh. He had a key. With dames it was usually the things they didn't want to talk about that got them killed. It was usually the one they would swear could never hurt them, but they were trying real hard to get away from because their brain read things clearer than their heart.

He pulled a gat of his own. Some shiny chrome job bigger than my Colt 1911. Maybe he thought he was hunting bear, because that was a lot of gun for a sleeping broad. Of course, it wasn't going to be enough. Not this time.

He ghosted back to the closet.

"Show time, doll. One guy, one gun. Coming quiet. You don't make a sound until he makes his play. Then you shoot. Don't talk, don't think, and don't die!"

I gave her the hard stare; if she was going to freeze, I had to know. You can't tell sometimes, until the time comes, who's got the steel to finish, and who's going to fold. . . Her lips went white; her breathing got deep, but slowed down. Her thumb slowly pushed the gun off safe. Well now. I've seen worse. I winked at her, and faded back by the bed.

Her left hand gripped her necklace, some kind of half cross or upside down hammer. Her right was at shoulder height, ready to bring her piece down on target.

The jackass came through the door screaming. I cleared my piece, even thought I can't touch the living. Reflex, I guess. Any surprise he would have had was gone. He lowered that cannon and started to blast.

Five shots rang like trip hammers. Three sounded like shotgun blasts, the cannon jumping in jackass's hand like a scared rabbit. He put a hole about chest level in the woman shape under the covers, then another in the pillow beside where her head would lay, then at the top of her headboard. Whatever that cannon was, he couldn't control it, anymore than he could control his screaming. The last two shots were sharp cracks, as the muzzle flash from the doll's little gun snapped out a sharp double tap, and jackass hit the floor.

* * *

"Nobody leaves me, you bitch!" Joey screamed as he came in the door. Unloading his Desert Eagle and his hate towards the girl who dared to leave him. He blasted out three times before he felt something hit him, and he fell to the floor.

He struggled to roll over, and saw her. That little bitch! The one who left him, the one who had the balls to send the Sheriffs to serve him at work with a restraining order, as if it was up to her when it was over. His chest was cold, and his legs were weak, but he snarled as he raised his Eagle towards his woman, HIS woman, whatever anyone said.

Joey heard a cold voice say, "Finish it, sister, this kid isn't stopping."

Joey looked into those eyes that used to look at him with love, and the ones he taught to look at him with fear, but this time they were flat, cold, and looking back in the moonlight on either side of the glowing sights of her Glock. Two more shots rang out, and he heard his pistol hit the floor. He couldn't feel it. He couldn't feel anything.

* * *

"Joey," the dame said, and then started to cry. Let the kid cry. She had earned it. He felt the end coming; they were coming again. They always did.

Joey came out of his body, and reached for his gun. You could do that if you hated enough. I did.

"This isn't over," Joey sobbed, as he picked up his gun, and raised it towards his loved/hated ex. "This will never be over!" he screamed.

"Hey bub," rang a cold voice, edged with cruelty. "You want to bet on that?"

He spun to face the trenchcoated figure, shining moonlight silver in the darkness, but thunder spoke, and a hammer took him in the knee.

"My gun can't touch the living any more, but you should see what it does to the dead. You could have let it go, buddy, you could have let her go and lived."

The gun spoke again, and Joey screamed.

"Both legs—you will never rise, never walk."

Twice more the gun spoke, and Joey's shoulders were slammed to the floor.

"Both arms—you will not raise them to another woman."

Joey started to beg now; he was almost out of time. They both were.

The grim ghost looked down, his eyes shaded by his fedora. The muzzle of the .45 looked like a train tunnel, as the smoke from the first four rounds puffed like a dragon's breath around its muzzle. "And your head, because I'm tired of listening to you."

Joey faded into silence. A roughly man-shaped pool of silver in the darkness, without form, without movement, without hope. "Your choice to be stupid, my choice who lives."

He looked at the locked slide on his pistol, and released it. Slapping its empty form back into its holster, he turned to face what was coming. He lit a cigarette and sucked deep on it. He knew what was coming, If he could have run, he would. It hurt too much to remember, except at the end.

From the moonlight came Her. Shining the blonde came. Angie's mother. I wished I died this time first. Sometimes when I failed, I ate my gun before they came, and missed this part. Sometimes I wished I had failed at this point. Five rounds, that's all I had at the end.

She was smiling, the way she was when she fed me the spiked booze, and left me passed out while she handed her kid back over to the monster that paid for her, the one whose guys I took her from in the first place.

The kid's grandmother paid me to track Angie down, and I did. Two knuckle draggers for hire had grabbed her and were holding her at a hotel. Neither one was willing to face a drawn pistol for the money they were getting. Bottom feeders, not the kind that came back from war, or came up through the gangs.

I brought her back to the mother. The blonde. Her face was hard and cold when I brought her back, and she told Angie to go to her room while she made a phone call. I cooled my heels in the living room while she made the call. When she came back she was all smiles, and brought a drink. Her blouse was unbuttoned enough to really distract me, and I never turned down good booze.

I never had much luck with broads and none with ones as hot as this one. I tried to play it cool, but my brain shut off as she ran her hands on my chest, and told me to finish my drink.

When I came to, I was passed out in the chair with a headache. Angie was gone, her mother too. I staggered to the girl's room; it looked like a fight happened. Angie was a fighter, she didn't go easy. I saw a button on the ground. Her mothers. Her mothers.

Played like a fool. Her mother sold her, just like the last time. Two mooks too scared to face me didn't snatch the kid themselves, they got her drugged unconscious by her mother, only this time she used it on me.

Booze and broads, I never could turn them down, and this time a kid was paying. Angie.

I called the operator, gave them my old badge number, and got the last number called. Lassiter. Old Man Lassiter.

Lassiter was old money, bought judges and congressmen out of petty cash, and was untouchable. We all knew about him, and the rumors about his tastes. Nobody ever linked him directly to the bodies; nobody ever looked that hard, or else they were warned off. Nobody ever went after him.

I rubbed my head and my eyes fell upon the bottle. Well, I guess I just proved I was a nobody, a real chump.

I cleared my pistol and blasted the bottle and glass. Two rounds out of seven spent. Five left.

"Angie baby, I swear I'm going to get you back, Hell take anybody who gets in the way."

117

My Ford weaved all over the road as I shook off the Mickey Finn. I clipped a mirror on the gatepost on the way in, and went through the shrubs on his pretty lawn.

I came up the stairs at a run, Colt in my fist.

Two guards were at the door and reached for me. Amateurs. I didn't waste a bullet on either of them. I knocked mustache boy's coconut off the door post, and pistol whipped the second mook. I didn't slow down. You crossed the wire at the run, and didn't stop until you hit the opposite trench. Slow was dead. Dead was OK, but only after I finished. Only I after I saved Angie.

I hit the stairs at the run; there was a butler in a stupid costume. He clawed at a piece behind his back. The stupid suit made him slow, my .45 made him stop forever. Four left.

Another stood at the top of the stairs, and got off two shots of his own. One hit my chest, I felt cold, but it wasn't enough. It threw off my aim, and my return splashed his throat into a red mess. Three left.

I came through the door, and there she was. Angie's mom, her purse was grasped in her hand, and she shot a look at the bedroom door. I heard a little girl screaming, and the wet slap of a man's hand stopped it. I put a bullet just above those sweet red lips. Couldn't let her speak, they made a fool of me before, and I may already be too late. Two left.

I hit the door, kicking beside the lock, not with my shoulders because the movies got it wrong. My vision was starting to grey out, not a good sign. Did I have enough time? I would have to.

Lassiter was kneeling over Angie. His pants were down, and he had his hands at her throat. I put a bullet in his spine, but the old bastard got up again.

I was on the ground, I didn't notice falling. It was cold, and my vision was graying out. Not good. The old bastard raised himself up, and reached for the girl again. I put my last round through his temple, and blew his brains all over the antique bed drapes.

I couldn't move now. I heard the screams of the mansion staff, heard soft sobbing from somewhere.

"I didn't make it Angie, I let you down. I swear I'll make it right."

From the shadows of the bed came two figures. One was a horror, half her face bloated and rotten, half cold and beautiful. Both her eyes were hungry as they looked at me. You see strange things at the end. I looked away from her, and there she was, the blonde; Angie's mom, the vision of beauty seemed to have gotten over the slug through the skull, and was smiling at me too. I shut my eyes. Some things I just couldn't face.

"Mine," said the blonde.

"Not yet," said the two faced horror.

It was a mercy when the dark came. It never lasted, but I welcomed it at the end.

It was the new dame that shattered the memory. She turned to my specters as if she saw them too, and shouted two names.

"Hella!" she said, raising her arm in salute to the dark one, her eyes unafraid as she took in the two faces of the cold dark. The dark one nodded in return.

"Freya," she said saluting the blonde. That wasn't Angie's mother's name, but the blonde laughed and nodded in return.

This had never happened. Not even I knew who they were; just that they came for me, at the end. Nobody saw them but me.

Who was this girl, and how did she know his specters?

* * *

It was hard to think, standing over the body of her dead ex, but the shock of the killing was nothing compared to the coming of the goddesses. Hel was cold, her presence deep in ways that spoke of the mound, of eternity. Her coming swept away shock and fear, for hers was a presence that anchored deep in the roots of the earth, and beyond.

At her glance, the silver pool that was the sundered essence of her attempted killer sunk into the floor, and the slight smile on her face was like moonlight on a bared blade. The look she turned upon her defender, the trench-coat clad ghost, was softer; if not kind, then at least understanding. When she looked at how her specter faced the keeper of the dead, she was shocked to see him flinch, not from the half-corpse grave-queen, but from the Goddess of Love.

Freya was hard to look upon; her light was bright, not as sunlight, but as fire; amber and gold. Her beauty was vibrant, wild and fierce; even still, she had the quality of dance, as if she was but a frozen moment between frenzied steps. Her gaze upon the ghost was warm. In those eyes shone understanding, love, and a fierce possessive desire. Not the desire of a lover, so much as the desire to possess, the need to have something discovered.

Her specter turned on trembling legs of ghost-silver away from the shining light of Freya, and towards the corpse-queen's dark. At last Freya's gaze fell upon her, and the goddess spoke.

"Kitten, would you know why he flees me? Would you know what he sees?"

I nodded; I could not speak under that gaze.

"Then see his memories, look at the things he won't see. He has earned more than he allows himself. He has won more than the task he sets himself. There is a place for him in other halls than the mound."

Freya looked at the specter with sad eyes.

"For him I wear the face of her that he first saved, but he sees only the mother. His generation had forgotten us. Many won great worth, but even some of those were lost, and need a guide to find their way home."

Those last words fell upon me like a great weight. As her eyes met mine, I saw the visions that haunted, that trapped my specter. As he lay dying upon the ground, I saw a young girl, shining golden with the promise of beauty to come, rush to his side, and weeping, close his eyes. When the police came, she told them, weeping, of his heroism. She heard the echo of a name. . . Angie.

He didn't know! He had been condemning himself for generations for failing her, but he didn't fail. He was not running from the woman he killed (she shuddered at the thought of a mother selling her child to that fate), but from the child he saved!

A gift for a gift, she thought, looking at the bullet holes in her bed; she had been given the gift of life. She looked at her ghost, the haunted look in her haunt's own eyes. She owed a life, but how was she to pay it back? She looked at Hel, and for the living to meet that dread gaze was harder than looking down the barrel of her pistol at her former lover. Turning from the light, to face the silver shadow in the heart of the dark, Kat turned to face Hella.

As she met the gaze of the two-faced queen, Hel turned the corpse face she showed the living. Staring at the corpse bloat and milky eye of the keeper of the dead, Kat steeled herself and met Hel's gaze. "Great Hel, I beg a question."

Hel turned her maiden face to the hard-faced ghost, fumbling to light a cigarette for whatever comfort it offered the dead. A soft smile touched the Keeper of Silence, and she asked a question in a voice that was soft as a lullaby.

"For the champion?"

Freed to speak when the Dread Queen turned to look at the smoking specter, Kat mumbled her assent.

"He is not mine to keep. He will not rest. Those that are mine know rest, an end to strife. He flees to me, and I wrap him in my darkness, but always the call will come, and his guns and wrath, not my arms, will hold him."

The Keeper of the Dead turned her corpse face to the living once more and spoke her last.

"He is not mine to keep."

It was times like this the sagas had great words from inspired poets. Too bad she was standing in her closet in her pajamas, standing over a body, looking at two goddesses, and trying to save a ghost. Sadly, this did not make for poetry.

"Shit," said Kat. She stripped the mag from her pistol, clearing and safing it. Checking the chamber was clear, she worked the slide lock and put down the empty gun. It was time to finish things; she thought she heard sirens already.

Quick and dirty heathen 101 or ghost intervention. It was now or never.

"A gift for a gift," she said. "I don't have a lot of time, the police are coming, but there is something you need to know."

* * *

The darkness was lapping around me now, the cold black promise of oblivion, the chance to forget. I could feel the blonde behind me, feel her calling to me. One day I might be weak enough to give in. I gave in once, and Angie died. I died too, but I couldn't even get that right. I turned to the dark lady again, her smile was cold and hard as a drawn knife, she knew me, and she knew what came next. The cold, the silence. . . the call again.

"Shit"—the dame I saved had a mouth on her like a platoon sergeant, but she shot straight, and didn't flinch, so I guess she was alright. She said she had something I needed to know, but she was wrong. Stuff only mattered to the living; it only mattered until you got the big one wrong, then you were screwed for life. Or death in my case. You screwed up the big one, you paid and paid, and even a bullet couldn't get you out.

I smiled, the darkness was drawing back. The dark lady wanted me to listen, and I guess the kid earned a minute. Being dead, my time got cheaper than a plug nickel.

"You never remember the end," she said.

No kidding. I got played for a sucker, and Angie died. I got the broad that sold her and the fat cat who bought her. The torpedoes didn't count; they were nothing, so was I. I didn't save Angie, and even if I got it right a few times, I failed when it counted, I failed when I died, because so did she.

The sirens were getting closer, the kid seemed desperate. She stepped away from her gun, and looked like she wanted to slap me. I get that a lot, or did when I had a body to slap.

"No, you idiot!" Kid had a silver tongue, all right.

He chuckled, but the kid had her motor running and shifted gears like she had places to go.

"You died, but she didn't. The crying you heard was Angie—she lived. She was crying and closing your eyes when the police got there. That's not her mother's face you see behind you, that's Angie when she grew up."

The dark lady looked sad; her eyes were almost soft as she nodded. Eyes like that couldn't lie; they never tried. Death didn't cheat; she was the one unbroken promise. He didn't know much, but he knew that.

The sirens grew loud, as they did that night when he was fading out. He heard then from a child, what he heard now from the blonde, so beautiful it hurt, so bright she burned.

"You came back for me. I knew you would. You are a hero. There is a place for heroes. My lady keeps it. You don't have to go into the dark. You can come again when you are called."

The kid seemed to understand. I didn't. I turned to her, because she played it straight so far, and I wasn't trusting myself to think, not with her in front of me.

"Go with her." The dame was smiling and crying the way only dames could. "Freya's hall is for heroes and lovers." I looked at the empty clip in my 45 and the spot the ghost died again and laughed.

"I ain't a hero, doll face. And if there is a bigger fool at love than me, I never met him."

My voice turned hard and cold, I knew how it played out. How it always played out.

"Out of bullets, out of time. Now the dark comes."

A golden laugh lit the darkness, and I felt the shiver run up my spine like the caresses you dream about, but never know. My gun grew heavy in my hand; I stripped the clip and counted. One, two, three. . . seven? NO! I wasted two, and since I died, I only had five left, like when I tried to save her. Seven slugs looked back at me, and I looked up to three smiles.

The kid was crying, the dark one nodded and turned away, and.

122

. . Angie took my arm. I felt a rush, like blood and fire pour through me, like a living man, like whiskey and a first kiss, and dawn after a night of war. I looked down at the ghost of my arm, and saw it fade.

* * *

Kat watched Hel turn away, and the amber tones of life fill the bone-white hollows of the dead man's face. Love hid behind walls of fear in his eyes, but wonder made him look at Angie, and see love shining back in return.

A gift for a gift, a life for a life.

Standing alone in a room with no ghosts and a single dead body, she heard the police come in and she began to laugh. This was actually going to be the easy part of her evening. Tears streaking her face, she sat back in the closet to wait. There had been enough truth for the evening. Her ghost prepped her for the coppers, and a little damsel in distress beat the hell out of telling the local flat-feet about goddesses and ghosts. Gods, now he had her talking like that. Next thing you knew, she would be smoking. . .

Chapter 4: After Death

Lessons of a Hammer

I can guarantee there is life after death. No promises it will be yours, or mine for that matter, but we will leave others behind us. We are given only one guarantee in the lore about death from the Hávamál:

Cattle die, and kinsmen die,
And so one dies one's self;
One thing now that never dies,
The fame of a dead man's deeds.

So death may or may not be the end for us individually, even if we are absolutely sure we are done with the standard issue flesh, quantity one, we are issued at birth. We are more than the flesh we wear, we extend beyond our skin, as we are not alone in it. We are connected, each to the other by the ties we forge in life, by the way our wyrd, the line of our life and luck tangle our lines with those lives we have touched, and who have touched us. We are a stone thrown in an ocean. We pass for a small time through the air before passing the depths and the dark claims us. Our passage has as much effect as we have made our passage, our life, our words and our deeds matter and connect us to each other. The ripples from a small stone may touch the shores of distant continents and reflect back again and again, to echo for centuries, as the effects you had on the lives you touched cause them to affect the lives of those you never knew in life. We are our deeds, our worth is measured in what we do, what we say, and how we honour our relationships. How much of that worth is visible is an interesting question. How much of it we see, or how much of what we see is real is another one. Those who think themselves connected to none may simply not be aware of the importance they have, or have had in the lives of others. We speak of wyrd as a weave because we are all connected to each other, the living, the dead, and the yet to be born. What the Norns know of us, we may not know. What Odin and Frigg know of the weavings we have only speculation on. All that we know for sure is that while we live, we see too small a portion of our effect to ever judge honestly what they may be. Legacy is something that you may work your life to build but no man or woman living knows, or can know, what will be after their passage.

Sometimes a passage that we think should pass unnoticed will rock our world. So it is with humanity that not all of our bonds are visible. So it is with the gods and ancestors; those who do not stand inside the weave any more, may see more deeply the connections we should be caring for.

What is it that we leave behind? How will it affect those who come after, and what role have our gods and ancestors in watching those whose trusted support lies now in the grave?

Scott was dying. This is not what he dreamed about when he came back from war to start a family, start a business, but wyrd weaves as it will. He had Tammy, a good woman to walk beside him all the days of his life; I guess they both thought that would last a little longer, but cancer is no great respecter of plans.

His boy was a fine strong boy, but he would grow up without a father, and without a father's lessons. Granted, Scott wasn't much for listening when his father was talking, but he learned a lot working with him, a lot he never really appreciated until he grew to manhood in the Army and realized how his father, who had so little skill with words, had taught him so much not with language, but with the lessons in his workshop, the lessons of the work they shared, the lessons of the hammer.

Looking down at his hands, once so strong, now too weak to even lift his hammer, he looked inside himself, and whispered a prayer. "Thor watch over my son, when I cannot. Let Tammy know she is doing a good job when it gets too much." Staring at the end, he whispered, "I wish he could learn the lessons of the hammer like I did." His watch done, his thread run full length, he joined his ancestors without fanfare or farewell.

Dave was ten and tired of other people telling him how he should act. He was not his mother to face each problem with deep emotions, nor was he like the counsellors at school, endlessly thinking about, and droning on about, his feelings. He didn't know how he was supposed to act, but he knew none of them were going to show him either. Dad and Grandad were dead and gone, and their ghosts were standards he could never live up to, and probably 90% BS anyway. He had his friends, he had hockey, and he had his video games. He really loved the swords and sorcery stuff. Nothing like smashing trolls with an axe or hammer to make you feel right in the world.

It was his birthday, and his mom had texted that she had a special present from his great-uncle, something special. Probably lame. His great-uncle was an old coot who talked funny.

The present was as long as his arm, and wide enough for a laptop. Heavy too. He opened it, and inside was a scarred hammer, an old carpentry tool that looked long enough to hammer a railroad spike through a redwood. Old iron marks and odd scars marred its surface, and the grip was worn by the passage of hands many thousands of times. The card read simply: "This was your father's, and his father's before him. It knows things you need to learn."

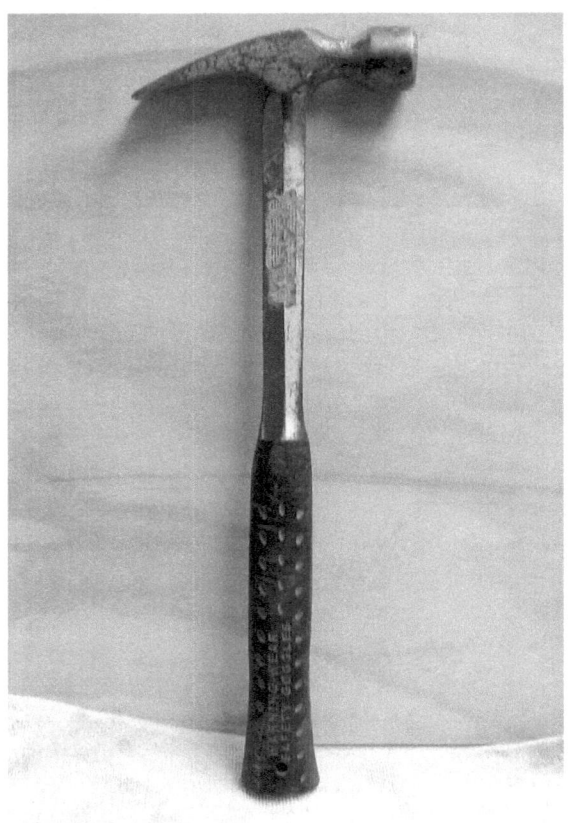

His mother held it in her hands like it was a holy relic. She fought back the tears and told him he should take it to his room and keep it with him. What junk. This wasn't any kind of hammer he wanted. He took it to his room and threw it on the bed. Taking up his controllers, he activated his game. Taking up his Warhammer, it crackled with caged lightning and he walked into the mountains to battle trolls and ogres, winning fame and fortune. . . and enough XP to unlock the next quest.

Dinner time came, and he decided to ditch the hammer. All game long, he felt the damned thing was looking at him. Watching him, almost like a person. It felt like mom used to make him feel when she would sneak into his room to watch him when he was sleeping. Not saying anything, just standing there smiling as he drifted off. He wasn't five anymore, and things without eyes shouldn't look at you. This was going in Chang's Palace dumpster (the Chinese restaurant down the block). Sticking bunches of crap that piled up in his room (yeah, yeah, really should clean. . .) into a garbage bag, he stuffed the hammer in too. "Taking out the trash mom!" he shouted. His mother looked surprised and pleased. Whatever. He did clean up sometimes, even if she didn't think so.

In the rear of the restaurant, a man was talking on his cell phone leaning up against a big work truck with huge tool cabinets on the side, covered with explosive markers. I guess it was a Dodge, because there were two ram logos on the front, rather than the usual one, and the sides were marked "Thunder Pyrotechnics Inc." It looked like a movie prop truck, you saw them when they were going to blow stuff up when film crews worked the area. What a cool job! Giving the big guy his space, Dave went to throw the garbage bag into the dumpster, but the claw of the hammer had already torn the bag, and when he tossed the bag, the hammer flew out and struck the parked truck with an alarming clang.

Dave froze. The big man hung up his cellphone, and size twelve work boots stomped around the corner of the van, and a huge scarred paw of a hand picked up the hammer, which looked oddly right in the large mans hand. He made happy grumbling noises as he swung it gently, and seemed to close his eyes and just listen for a moment.

"That's a pretty nice hammer you have there, son. Why would you throw it out?"

Dave muttered something about how lame a hammer it was, and the big man just grinned behind his beard. He reached into his truck, and pulled a movie prop out of it. It was a real Warhammer.

Scarred and brutal, it looked like it should be crushing giant skulls or smashing shields. It looked better than the one he used in his game.

The big man scratched his beard for a bit while he balanced both hammers in his right palm, as if they weighed nothing.

"Tell you what, kiddo. I know what each of them can do, but I bet you don't. Why don't you tell me which one you want, and if you still feel that way in a week, you can keep it."

Well duh, trade a lame used tool for a movie weapon! Done deal dude.

The man left his card, and just to be polite Dave tucked it into his jacket pocket. It's not like he was going to need it , right?

The next day he took it out back to play. He swung the hammer as hard as he could at the half wall the city was tearing down from the old Church. He wanted to feel what it was like to smash a shield for real. The hammer seemed to speed up on its own when he swung and it shattered the brick wall like it was glass. Brick exploded everywhere, and Dave was nursing a dozen cuts from little fragments. That was COOL. He imagined smashing trolls or giants with that, and he was just like the heroes of the game. The hammer made him feel like a hero!

Throwing the hammer at the back wall (like his character could do as soon as he "levelled up"), he saw the hammer fly like a rocket and smash through the back wall, before hammering back into his hand hard enough that he dropped it and spent several minutes trying to get his hand to work again. What the hell! That was NOT normal.

Deciding he needed to go home and think for a bit, he hung the hammer from his backpack and started walking home. On the way he saw Abigail. She was a nice girl from up the block. She was slow, retarded or something. Sweet as could be, but not much more than a kid, even if she was as old as Dave's babysitters. Abigail was crying. She was holding a birdhouse whose roof had come apart, and the chain to hang it had come loose.

"Hey, Abby, what's wrong?" Dave asked her quietly, because she was crying, but trying not to show it. When you are not as fast as the other kids, not as smart, you are easy for people to pick on, and you learn early to hide when they made you cry.

Abigail turned towards Dave with the broken birdhouse. "I made this in class for the birds to live in, so the cats can't get at them. Tommy from up the street, he threw basketballs at it until it broke, and I don't have a hammer to put it back together again. Do you have a hammer?"

Dave felt his hand tighten on the hammer hanging from his backpack. He didn't like the idea of people picking on Abigail, and thoughts of using this hammer filled his mind. Abby looked down at the hammer in hope, and Dave's thoughts crashed back to earth. This hammer swung like a wrecking ball, it would smash her birdhouse the rest of the way.

"I'm sorry, Abby. My hammer doesn't know how to do that."

Dave remembered his father hammering little tiny nails into the wall to put up the trim, the hammer stroking more like a magician's wand than a brutal hunk of steel. A single gentle tap, just enough to drive it in, and not a mark left behind. But this wasn't that kind of hammer. It couldn't teach that.

"Hey, it's the half wit and her doll house!"

It was the mocking voice of Tommy from up the block. He was twelve, about four inches taller and twenty pounds heavier than Dave. Seeing the fear in Abbigail's eyes, he knew he would stand anyway. The hammer at his side quivered with the need to be used. Dave looked at it in sick fear. Remembering the smashing walls, the visions of smashed troll skulls changed to broken teenage boys bleeding on the ground, Dave wanted badly to throw up. This was that kind of hammer. This was not what he wanted. He remembered his mother talking about why Dad had joined the

Army when she first met him. "He didn't like to fight, honey, but sometimes you see something that is wrong, and you just can't do nothing about it. You have to take a stand." That he could do.

Dave turned to Abigail, "Abby, can you hold this for me? It's not mine, and I don't want to lose it."

She looked at him with big eyes. He was going to get his butt kicked. He wasn't going to kill a boy over a birdhouse, but you don't just let someone like Abby get picked on and do nothing. You have to take a stand.

Stepping between Abby and Tommy, Dave raised his fists and shook out his shoulders. He played hockey and knew how to put his body behind a hit. Bigger or not, if Tommy wanted to get past Dave, he was going to pay for it. "Big guy, Tommy, making Abby cry, smashing her birdhouse."

A group of Tommy's friends was wandering over from the ball courts to look at the fight. One of them was about six inches taller than Dave, and wide as two of him. He was scowling as he came, looking angry.

Dave stood his ground, and when Tommy went to step forward, the bigger boy from the basketball court grabbed Tommy and pushed him against the wall.

"Tommy you punk, what the hell you do to Abby?" The big kid apparently knew Abby too. "She's my cousin you dweeb. You touch her again and I'll flatten you."

Abby smiled at Dave and her cousin as the other kids wandered off, no longer interested if a fight wasn't breaking out. Abby went to hand back Dave's hammer and both of them froze, because the heavy Warhammer was gone, and in its place was a scarred, worn carpenter's hammer, as long as Dave's forearm. Her eyes smiling, she looked at Dave and said, "Can you fix the birdhouse now, Dave?"

Picking up the hammer in his hands and swinging it in the slow gentle stroke he remembered from his father he answered truthfully. "Yes, my hammer knows how to do that."

When he got back home, after hanging the repaired birdhouse to Abbigail's satisfaction with the help of her much taller cousin, Dave looked in his jacket for the card with Donnar's number on it. Where the number was, there was now simply a note:

"Good choice kid, that hammer has lots of lesson left in it."

The hammer stayed on his dresser from then on. It saw a lot of use, and somehow, Dave just felt better knowing that when it was there, someone was watching out for him. The hammer came from his father, and his father before him. The hammer had learned from each generation of his family, and now it was left to him. They weren't there to teach him themselves, but inside the hammer was all they ever taught it, and when he used it, he swore he could hear their voices giving the lessons, and almost feel their hands guiding him still.

Barren

The ancestors are worthy of praise and remembrance, and receive their due from us. Death is no more equal than life is, and the Disir receive special veneration for a few good reasons. The Disir are the maternal ancestral spirits, literally the females of your line who guide and guard it still. This is not simply your direct ancestors, but all the women of your line. The Norse and Germans often gave offerings to the Disir or Matronae right before battle, as they knew that not only did their maternal ancestors watch over them, but unlike the male ancestors, their death did not end their power to affect the world. Even into Christian times, offerings were made to the Disir, as they were deemed to hold real power to affect this world, and a real interest in advancing the interests of their family.

Dís is a title, like "wight," that oddly enough applies equally to the living and the dead: you could become recognized as a Dis in your life through your role in the family. We are all connected, through birth, through adoption, through marriage, through oath, through the reciprocal gifting relationships we forge in life, however we name them. All of these ties are real, all are sacred, and few of them indeed are affected by so small a thing as death. Death is the silence at the end of the song, but the song lives on, and its echoes can reach across the ages. What we did in life touches more lives than our own, and can well bring change into the lives of others you never met. To stand at the end of your life and know what you have accomplished is hubris. You can only see your own thread. Who but the gods can see all the lives you touched? All the threads crossed or tied to yours, all the patterns changed because of how your thread has drawn upon others?

There are those who look upon what they sought to do in life, and never attained, and judge that they have failed to change the world as they wished. Perhaps it is only after we are gone that we can truly see the difference some people have made in the lives of many. By our deeds we will be known, but little can we know the worth that others held our deeds. Life is largely made up of the thousand little things you do waiting for great events to occur. Change is likewise born of a thousand little things added to one side of your scales or another, as your balance between success or failure may sometimes be decided by the shadow of a feather. How often has someone been that feather on the scales, for good or ill, that decided all?

The party had been wonderful. Norma had no children of her own. For all that she had "known" that was her purpose growing up on the farm in Alberta, it had proved not to be the case. No children for her; she was barren. Still, she had a lot of love in her heart, and when her best friend, indeed a woman who had grown closer than her own sister, had fallen to a heart attack and left behind two small children, she did what she could, what Aillie would have.

Christine and Suzie were good girls, grown now, and Christine had a husband and three girls of her own now, but they still came here for their birthdays, Easter, and Thanksgiving. Their stepdad tried when their mom died, but he was a good provider, a good father, but not very good at occasions. Norma was, so she stepped in and hosted for them.

She was tired, sat down on the hearth to rest for a bit. There was Alyssa's bunny. The littlest girl, she never got a chance to play with the Teddy Bear Norma kept for her two older sisters and the other children she hosted here, so Norma bought a little blue bunny that was just for Alyssa when she was here. Alyssa always left it at the hearth when it was time to go, but it was glued to her, inside the house or out, all the time she was there. Norma smiled. She wished Aillie could have seen her grandchildren. She wished she could have had her own, but she was barren, and would leave nothing behind her when she was gone. She was so tired. She would just close her eyes here and rest until Earl got back from the track, then she would clean up. She loved hosting parties, but she was just so tired. . .

* * *

The news hit everyone hard. Aunty Norma was dead. Granted, she was not "technically" an Aunty, only the oldest friend of their mother who had died when they were small. Norma had been one of the pillars of their world. Dad moved when his job required it, and was away at camp half the time. Older stepsiblings were teenagers or young parents themselves, and took care of the girls as best they could between their other commitments, but it was always Norma who was there for birthdays, Christmas, any special occasion or accomplishment. When they went to university, and even when Christine had her own family, they still all came to Norma's for occasions; it was what brought the family together.

Years came and went, and life moved on.

Christine heard that Roy and Teresa's child had cancer. Oh my gods. What a terrible thing. What could you do about something like that? Teresa was a wreck, she spent half her time at the hospital, and Roy was balancing his work and looking after their other daughter too. Their lives were coming apart, and there was nothing anyone could do.

Christine looked across her kitchen and saw her Corningware. When Norma's neighbor had cancer, there was nothing anyone could do, but Norma knew that Jeanie prided herself on her house, and on cooking for her husband. He was in bad shape spending half his time at the hospital, and the rest at work or dealing with their grown kids (and grandkids): trying to be strong for everyone else was killing him. Norma did what her mother trained her to do, and took care of the little things. She cooked full sizes of her recipes. Raised on a farm with eight kids, she cut everything down to cook for her and Earl; it was less trouble to cook the old way, and walk the bulk of the food across the street to her neighbor in Tupperware. He had good meals he could reheat, and she could straighten out the house a bit for Jeanie while she was over there. You couldn't fix cancer, but you could take care of the little things while your friends and neighbors faced the big ones.

Christine took out the big Corningware pots. She knew she had Norma's recipe book around here somewhere. Maybe she couldn't help Roy and Teresa, but she could make sure Roy and their other daughter had good food to eat at home, and make sure that she took the daughter to school when she ran her own kids to and from. That she could do. Like Norma said, you can't fix cancer, but you could take care of the little things while your friends and neighbors faced the big ones.

Years came and went, and life moved on.

Alyssa was the smallest, but smallest and small are not the same. Easter was coming, and she remembered the magic of the Easter Egg hunts at Norma's. She remembered as well Norma inviting the immigrant kids who came from Senegal and didn't have the custom there. Their parents were eager to share with them all of Canadian Culture, but how do you show what you don't know? Norma was there to help. She brought them into our family gatherings, and they learned to share the magic with the other kids, even as the parents learned to make the magic themselves. Alyssa was older now, and had rabbits of her own for real, but she kept the blue bunny she inherited after Aunty Norma died. She still believed in the Easter Bunny; not just her bunny named Easter, but in the magic of Ostara, the magic of Easter. It was not finding out the magic wasn't real when you grew up, it was finding out how the magic was made, and deciding for yourself if you wanted to make the magic live for others.

There were always people moving in and moving out of the townhouse complex; it was a three-bedroom suburban community with a big playground, and many families came and went, and now Alyssa was one of the big kids. There were a lot of little kids here who didn't come from Canada. Pilipino, Hungarians, and even a family that was raised "Jo Ho," whatever that meant. They didn't know all the traditions that made Easter important or fun. Looking from her live bunny, to the little blue bunny she inherited from Aunty Norma, she knew what Norma would do.

Alyssa conspired with Kelsey with bemused parental support, as they pooled their money and creativity to put on an Easter for all ages for the nearly fifty units with kids in the complex. Granted they went over budget and needed some parental help when they found out that two of the boys in the complex had serious nut allergies, and they had to stock some more expensive guaranteed nut-free candy for them, but it all came together. Year after year, a new tradition was build around the complex, more of the older kids joined in helping to put it on. When her father told her that what she had created would probably survive after she graduated and left, Alyssa just nodded and said "Just like Aunty Norma."

Caitlyn was brash and loud, but wore her heart on her sleeve. She could not wait to grow up and move out, but holiday time was depressing for those who were alone, far from home, and broke. Caitlyn listened to all her people at work complaining about how depressing it was to be alone at Christmas, which should have been funny as half of the workers at this store were born in India. Being the quiet and reserved girl that she was (not!), she loudly proclaimed that they were not without their family, they worked together every day, they shared what was going on in their lives, they were their own family, even the annoying ones. They should celebrate together. They were not going to be open for Christmas Eve anyway, even though they had to be in the store for a cleaning shift. Why not have the rest of the staff come in for a bit during the closed cleaning shift and spend it together?

From the back room came their manager, with an odd look on her face. She looked at everyone, and then disappeared into her office.

The next shift Caitlyn arrived at work, and the girl on till said "Go see Gurprit in her office."

Oh crap, the manager wants to see her. What had she done? Heck, she wasn't even late! As she clocked in, she looked at the notice board.

Staff Christmas Party: Dec 24
Organized by Caitlyn

Crap. Me and my big mouth. As she opened the door, the manager and the owner were talking. The manager smiled, and the owner took out his wallet and handed over a wad of cash, "For the party." Caitlyn smiled, nodded, and wished she could control her mouth. Here she was, sixteen, and tasked with organizing the company Christmas party for a company that had never even done one!

She was smiling and putting on her headset, while despairing about what she could possibly do, when she remembered Norma, dear sweet deeply Christian Aunty Norma, doing her best to get the decorations right for Heathen Ostara for her grand-nieces (sort-of-kind-of-by-adoption or something). She always had games to play, prizes, tons of baked goods, and weirdly enough, always some sort of jellied salad. Her parents said it was something from the 1970s, but it always struck the girls as deeply weird and deeply Norma. It was time to get her Norma on.

Grabbing one of her co-workers with a car, she said. "We are going shopping. I have a list. We are going to have lots of baked goods, we are going to play games, we are going have candy, and we are, by the gods, going to have jello molds!"

The party was a great success, and the invention of the Santa Claus Jello mold jello shooter (which she was too young, everyone reminded her, to actually try) were a hit. OK they were made from old Santa shaped ice cube trays her parents had, but they made wicked jello shooters, and they were now going to be a staff party holiday tradition. Somewhere, Caitlyn was sure, Norma was either smiling or wincing; she wasn't exactly sure which, but somehow she knew Norma would approve. People needed each other. They just needed someone to show them how to help.

In the mound there is silence and peace, and an end to cares. The dead rest easy in the mound. The female ancestral spirits, the disir, sleep as well, but lightly. The hand that rocks the cradle is the hand that rules the world, it was once said. True or not, the hands that guided those first steps will always be over our own in guidance. The words given to us by those who loved and guided us in life will sound in our ears long after those who spoke them are in the mound. To be a dis, a guardian of the line, does not come with childbirth, does not come with blood alone, or even necessarily come with blood at all. To be a dis in life is to bind yourself in life to those you care for, by the love you show, and the effort you put in to aiding them. To be a dis is not a thing that death can touch. The disir care little for death, for love and memory are not death's subjects.

The ancestors offered to their disir in life with the understanding that they had both the power and the inclination to help them still. We hear the words of our disir. Do we hear them speaking from beyond the grave, or do we simply recall the gift of their words given to us while they had the chance, that return to us when we have the need? Either way, it is a gift given, and must be matched with a gift in return. Since the gift was given by one who is passed, we must give in turn to others who yet live. In this way, the hands of the disir still work magic in the lives of the people. Not stage magic, not spells and sorcery magic, but the kind of magic that turns the hands and hearts of the living to the work of helping each other, as we were guided by our honored disir to do. This is a legacy death cannot touch. This is real.

Chapter 5: Gods and Guests

Gods at Kubb: Trothmoot 2014

They Walk With Us, but they don't lead us on strings. What they have left behind is not a book of laws to be obeyed, or a single right way to be a man, or a woman. Indeed, the many and conflicting natures of the gods themselves make it impossible for us to point to one and say that this is what we should all be!

What they left for us instead was instruction on how to look at the world, and our place in it. What they left us was a way for us to ask the right questions, and tools that we might take up, should they be useful in whatever means we have taken as our own to meet our challenges. We call on them to be with us, we call on them to point us in the right direction, even as we ask our ancestors for advice, but the challenges are our own, as are the victories, and the prices paid.

What if I don't hear them? I have heard this question from a thousand mouths, and before I answered, I honestly thought about those times the voices of the gods and ancestors were loud enough to be aware of and realized, they were only in times of great peril, or when on the edge of great mistakes. To have strayed enough from the path of prudence that you require a divine "clue by four" or wake-up call is not to be blessed. It is the same as any alarm; it is your last chance to correct an error before it becomes irrevocable. You would never ask if your car didn't love you because the check engine light never came on, or your home was ill-kept because your smoke detector never howled at you while you slept for no reason at all. So it is with the gods, I think. They walk with us, content to see what we do, and there to offer a whisper in the silence, a nudge at the fork in the road, and gentle laughter when we get it right, even though frequently we take strange paths indeed to get there.

It was the last night of moot, and the thunderstorms that had been forecast had lent only a touch of their winds to the day, and the crown of lighting that ringed the hilltop to highlight but not disturb the revellers. The hearthfire had been put out, and ashes smouldered in the silence when at last the waiting sky opened, and the rain and thunder drove the last sluggards to their cabins. Last night of moot, last night of magic.

The rain hammered down, but seemed to part around the golden-haired youth who strode from the fire pit. He hailed the hulking shape in the dining hall shadows with a voice of golden laughter.

"The land thanks you for your gift, Red Beard. I had not expected to see you here." The Red Beard stood with a guilty grin from where he crouched upon the stones before the dining hall.

"Well met, Alf-lord. They called me here when they made sport of my courtship with Sif."

In the hand of the Hammer Thrower, whose might shattered mountains and laid low jotnar, was a small blue stuffed bull, the size of a kitten. The rain that flowed o'er his brow and fire red beard touched not the little toy, with its ridiculous horns.

Frey regarded the bull in the hands of his kinsman and smiled to see the fearless one look abashed. With gentle humour he inquired, "Did they get it right?"

The question was one that rang in the halls beyond the world we know, as indeed those who hailed them now were much changed from those whose halting steps upon this world they once did guide. In many ways they had grown from helpless children into fractious youth. In many things they showed promise, in many others peril. Like any child, they railed against instruction as oft as seeking it, and sometimes took lessons from their trials that were different from what was sought to teach. They got much wrong, and yet, some right. In many things they got the details wrong, or lit upon ones of little meaning to hang much worth, and yet. . . and yet they stumbled on and on towards worth, towards community, towards health. In the play that called his eye they got much wrong, but it called to him, as they did, for in their fumbling towards memories long lost to them they found some truth. He smiled and answered. "They were close enough."

Frey's own hand was full as well, and Thor did ask, "Who called you, Herd-King, and what is it you hide in your own soft hand?" Frey laughed to hear his kinsmen flyte him so, and answered with equal mirth.

"Apple Pie Moonshine!" he laughed, extending the jar to his red-bearded kinsmen to sip. "Two are here that I had gifted. It seems the lad had made for me an image, and brought it in to overlook the marriage bed. Indeed their worship was so ardent that I brushed aside the mortal means of delay, and gave to them the gift they had not yet realized they wanted. At Freyfaxi was the birthing."

The two gods chuckled at mortals' odd ways, but kindly.

"I came because she called. I heard her song offered to the fire and the gathered folk, and far from the hearth I visited, so here I came. Motherhood had given depth to her voice, as fatherhood wholeness to the lad that pleases me much."

A gentle voice that wove between the hammering rain like branches reaching towards the sun did call. A woman strode, tall and swaying like a fruit tree heavy with blossom from the grove to the stones before the kitchen hall.

"Well wrought, Jotun-bane. Your rains have stilled the floating embers that touched my trees. Mortal eyes and hands do well, but the wights whispered of Muspel's fire. Pleased am I too, with what these folk have wrought, who took me for their own. Pleased as well with what they have done with my gifts."

140

Laughing, Thor passed the jar to his kinswoman with a smile. "Hail Idunna!"

The three turned as one, and gazed down at the cabin below. Idunna spoke with concern.

"Do you feel? They call the Battle-Glad! In a place of frith. . . "

Thor rumbled, unconcerned. "The glove is on the spear, the Leavings of the Wolf has pledged the peace that binds us all." His faith in his kinsmen was well known, but not as widely shared in the higher halls.

Frey looked long, and smiled. "They have not forgotten all, it seems. A volva is with them, old and wise is she, rooted deep. I see the raven mark on many here, and heavy the hand that brought them together. Whatever his ends, the Hanged One tends his blades with care. They learn what they must."

Idunna cast her eyes upon the stones and saw. . . a mortal strangeness. Five cans in red and white stood in a row, five cans of shining silver stood against them. A single can of green, a jotun among its kind, stood in the field center in all majesty. At first her thought was that this was mortal laziness, and when the Heron of Forgetfulness flew over the mead and beer consumed by men and god, they oft left their empty vessels where they lay. Littering, was the word in this land's tongue—but this looked done with a will, and to an end. Her curiosity roused, she sought the purpose of these matching battle lines of beer cans. "What mortal foolishness is this?" she asked.

Thor laughed. "Drunken Redneck Kubb!"

Kubb was a sport their children played, with wooden rods to cast at standing logs. It seemed that mortals in this tree-scarce place had sought to play with empty beer cans, and bottles with a tiny bit of water.

Frey laughed. "Is the point to drink or win?"

Thor was overcome with joy and right quickly explained the rules that caused a drink when an enemy toss succeeded, or your own toss missed, and how the struck kubbs were tossed back into play to keep the sport alive, that the taunts and jests and laughter should not swiftly be finished. The light of battle shone from his eyes, like the lightning in the sky above. First among the Vanir, in battle bold as in bed, Freyr felt his mirth swiftly rising, and swiftly did he bend and take a bottle up.

"This is no antler, but I like it well enough. What say you, goat-pulled As, will you match me without your hammer?"

Lightning crashed, and thunder voiced the joyous laughter. He picked up his water bottle as the sound of Njord's strong son's cast striking his first beer can thane rang loud in the rain-swept night.

"Drink deep, red beard! Beli's Bane will be your match!"

Thor looked with alarm upon the little jar, and cast his eye upon gentle Idunn. With a sigh, Idunna signed laguz above the Apple Pie Moonshine, that it ever flow. "I like the frith of this place well enough to tarry, but mark you, Storm Lord; your cloak of rain about us weave, that mortal eyes in mortal beds not be drawn to the boasting and laughter of fractious gods."

Thus it may have been, beneath the cloak of rain, that the most honoured guests of all did sport at Kubb.

Guest at the Feast

Old man walking in a long blue coat,
Hat slouched low in the shadow;
Cool gaze taking in the gathered folk
And the firelight shining in the meadow.

Picnic tables weighed down with food,
Children in knots scamper by;
Men and women laughing in joy
Beneath the stranger's cold eye.

"How are you called?" called a voice from the fire.
"Guest!" spoke a voice dry as dust.
Laughing, the old woman hailed him again,
"Come then and Guest then with us!"

Strange it seemed the garb that they wore,
Strange to see men sport with spears.
Women swirled past, bright-cloaked and bold-eyed,
Both to his taste, it appears.

"What do you here?" rasped a voice cold as iron.
"We honour the gods," her reply,
"Surely you jest," he crowed, now surprised,
As the challenge flashed bright in his eye.

A bearded man raised up his horn to the sky:
"The Æsir!" his shout to the sky.
The old woman took up the horn as it passed:
"The Vanir!" her ringing reply.

Laughing, a honey blonde took up the horn,
Necklace of gold lights her breast:
"The fallen!" Her voice is a warm wanton purr,
Her gaze boldly challenging Guest.

Grave-eyed, a boy came to Guest's left hand,
A sandwich he passed with a grin,
A horn to his right hand was topped up and passed.
For a moment his gaze turned within.

"Half a loaf you gave, and half a horn,"
He spoke, "yet full friend found.
"To the host!" with a voice loud as thunder;
One pull and the horn was downed.

Offerings made by the bold fire light,
Fellowship forged by the flame,
Mead and memories shared by the folk,
Kinsmen in all but the name.

Firelight falls and Guest whispers low,
In the ash he traces a sign.
Soon Guest and the honey blonde alone still awake,
Their smiles in the twilight do shine.

"Fare ye well," spoke Guest to the slumbering folk;
To the North he strode cross the lawn.
"Fare thee well," laughed the honey-gold maid,
Dancing her way towards the dawn.

For the Æsir, the Vanir, the wights of the lands and waters we share, our ancestors and honoured dead. You are all guests at our feasts. We thank you for sharing this journey with us.

—*John T. Mainer*

Illustration Sources

p. 3: http://zodiacmilpro.com/

p. 4: http://zodiacmilpro.com/

p. 9: Norse-mythology.org

p. 12: http://en.wikipedia.org/wiki/Ontario_Highway_401

p. 26: Parks Canada

p. 32: http://media.web.britannica.com/eb-media/07/93307-004-D76FD311.jpg

p. 37: John T Mainer, Heathen Freehold Society of British Columbia

p. 45: www.fredhutch.org/en/news/center-news/2013/10/what-not-to-say-to-a-cancer-patient/_jcr_content/articletext/textimage/image.img.jpg/1383236776964.jpg

p. 54: John T Mainer, Heathen Freehold Society of BC

p. 55: Viking Jack http://www.deviantart.com/print/19621445/

p. 56: stateeofdreaming https://www.tumblr.com/tagged/flaming-shots

p. 58: https://commons.wikimedia.org/wiki/File:Construction_worker_at_Westlake_Center,_1988.jpg

p. 58: http://wallpapers4u.net/thumbs/animals/red-chestnut-mare-legs-2221-480x320.jpg

p. 64: http://scandikitchen.typepad.com/scandikitchen/2011/01/ask-the-scandies-which-norse-god-is-coolest.html

p. 67: http://www.afghanistanacanadianstory.ca/content-accumulation/2007-2/

p. 69: http://screamingnorth.com/

p. 79: http://www.fotocommunity.de/pc/pc/display/18610136

p. 82: http://m.inmagine.com/image-dp1963833-Two-black-bear-cubs-following-their-mother-in-jasper-national-park;alberta%20canada.html

p. 83: "Bull Moose" by Robert Bateman

p. 87: https://darkjade68.files.wordpress.com/2011/10/elsya.jpg

p. 88: kurtisdawe

p. 89: http://www.emilybalivet.com/Cernunnos.html

p. 90: http://witcheri.blogspot.ca/2011/10/greek-gods-and-goddesses-iii.html

p. 94: "Poison Oak Greenman" by Liam Manchester

p. 96: https://enchantedamerica.files.wordpress.com/2014/08/ohio-kirkland-holden-arboretum-gnomes-5.jpg

p. 101: http://podcast.canadianmilitaryhistorypodcast.ca/?p=306

p. 108: Humphrey Bogart in *Bullets or Ballots* (William Keighley, 1936)

p. 111: http://fc01.deviantart.net/fs70/f/2011/274/d/8/hel_goddess_by_valkae-d4bhl3f.png

p. 116: Marlene Dietrich.
http://www.theplace2.ru/archive/marlene_dietrich/img/Marlene-Dietrich-769121.jpg

p. 128: Cergol Tool and Forge
https://www.facebook.com/cergolforge/photos_stream?ref=page_internal

p. 139: John T Mainer, Heathen Freehold Society of BC

p. 141: John T Mainer, Heathen Freehold Society of BC